RB✓

N

IN THE DRIVER'S SEAT

IN THE DRIVER'S SEAT

Stories

Helen Simpson

Alfred A. Knopf

New York / 2007

This Is a Borzoi Book
Published by Alfred A. Knopf

Knopf, Borzoi Books, and the colophon are registered trademarks
of Random House, Inc.

Originally published in Great Britain as Constitutional by Jonathan Cape,
an imprint of Random House Group Ltd., London, in 2005.

The stories in this collection have appeared in the following
publications: Brain Child Magazine, Candis Magazine, Granta,
The Guardian, Harper's Bazaar, The Independent, New Statesman,
Prospect Magazine, and Zoetrope: All-Story.

Library of Congress Cataloging-in-Publication Data
Simpson, Helèn, [date]
In the driver's seat : stories / by Helen Simpson.—1st American ed.
p. cm
"This is a Borzoi Book."
ISBN 978-0-307-26522-7
1. Middle-aged women—England—Fiction. 2. Domestic
fiction, English. I Title.
PR6069.I4226I58 2007

823'.914—dc22   2006037215

Manufactured in the United States of America
First United States Edition

Contents

IN THE DRIVER'S SEAT

Up at a Villa

They were woken by the deep-chested bawling of an angry baby. Wrenched from wine-dark slumber, the four of them sat up, flustered, hair stuck with pine needles, gulping awake with little light breaths of concentration. They weren't supposed to be here, they remembered that.

They could see the baby by the side of the pool, not twenty yards away, a furious geranium in its parasol-shaded buggy, and the large pale woman sagging above it in her bikini. Half an hour ago they had been masters of that pool, racing topless and tipsy round its borders, lithe Nick chasing sinewy Tina and wrestling her, an equal match, grunting, snaky, toppling, crashing down into the turquoise depths together. Neither of them would let go underwater. They came up fighting in a chlorinated spume of diamonds. Joe, envious, had tried a timid imitation grapple but Charlotte was having none of it.

"Get off!" she snorted, kind, mocking, and slipped neatly into the pool via a dive that barely broke the water's skin. Joe, seeing he was last as usual, gave a foolish bellow and launched his heavy self into the air, his aimless belly slapping down disastrously like an explosion.

After that, the sun had dried them off in about a minute, they had devoured their picnic of *pissaladière* and peaches, downed the bottles of pink wine, and gone to doze in the shade behind the ornamental changing screen.

Now they were stuck. Their clothes and money were heaped under a bush of lavender at the other end of the pool.

"Look," whispered Tina as a man came walking toward the baby and its mother. "Look, they're English. He's wearing socks."

"What's the matter with her now," said the man, glaring at the baby.

"How should I know," said the woman. "I mean, she's been fed. She's got a new nappy."

"Oh, plug her on again," said the man crossly, and wandered off toward a cushioned chaise longue. "That noise goes straight through my skull."

The woman muttered something they couldn't hear, and shrugged herself out of her bikini top. They gasped and gaped in fascination as she uncovered huge brown nipples on breasts like wheels of Camembert.

"Oh gross!" whispered Tina, drawing her lips back from her teeth in a horrified smirk.

"Be quiet," hissed Nick as they all of them heaved with giggles and snorts and their light eyes popped, overemphatic in faces baked to the color of flowerpots.

They had crept into the grounds of this holiday villa, one of a dozen or more on this hillside, at slippery Nick's suggestion, since everything was *fermé le lundi* down in the town and they had no money left for entrance to hotel pools or even to beaches. Anyway, they had fallen out of love over the last week with the warm soup of the Mediterranean, its filmy surface bobbing with polystyrene shards and other unsavory orts.

"Harvey," called the woman, sagging on the stone bench with the baby at her breast. "Harvey, I wish you'd . . ."

"Now what is it," said Harvey testily, making a great noise with his two-day-old copy of *The Times*.

"Some company," she said with wounded pathos. "That's all."

"Company," he sighed. "I thought the idea was to get away from it all."

"I thought we'd have a chance to *talk* on holiday," said the woman.

"All right, all right," said Harvey, scrumpling up *The Times* and exchanging his chaise longue for a place on the stone bench beside her. "All right. So what do you want to talk about?"

"Us," said the woman.

"Right," said Harvey. "Can I have a swim first?" And he was off, diving clumsily into the pool, losing his poise at the last moment so that he met the water like a flung cat.

"She's hideous," whispered Tina. "Look at that gross stomach, it's all in folds." She glanced down superstitiously at her own body, the high breasts like halved apples, the handspan waist.

"He's quite fat, too," said Charlotte. "Love handles, anyway."

"I'm never going to have children," breathed Tina. "Not in a million years."

"Shush," said Joe, straining forward for the next installment. The husband was back from his swim, shaking himself like a labrador in front of the nursing mother.

"'Us,'" he said humorously, wiggling a finger inside each ear, then drubbing his hair with the flats of his hands. "Fire away then."

She started immediately, as if she knew she had only two or three minutes of his attention, and soon the air was thick with phrases like Once she's on solids, and You'd rather be reading the paper, and Is it because you wanted a boy? He looked dull but resigned, silent except for once protesting, What's so special about bathtime? She talked on, but like a loser, for she was failing to find the appropriate register, flailing around, pulling clichés from the branches. At some subliminal level each of the eavesdropping quartet recognized their own mother's voice in hers, and glazed over.

"You've never moaned on like this before," marveled Harvey at last. "You were always so independent. Organized."

"You think I'm a mess," she said. "A failure as a mother."

"Well, you're obviously not coping," he said. "At home all day and you can't even keep the waste bins down."

Nick and Tina were laughing with silent violence behind the screen, staggering against each other, tears running down their faces. Joe was mesmerized by the spectacle of lactation. As for Charlotte, she was remembering another unwitting act of voyeurism, a framed picture from a childhood camping holiday.

It had been early morning, she'd gone off on her own to the village for their breakfast baguettes, and the village had been on a hill like in a fairy tale, full of steep little flights of steps, which she was climbing for fun. The light was sweet and glittering and as she looked down over the rooftops she saw very clearly one particular open window, so near that she could have lobbed in a ten franc piece, and through the window she could see a woman dropping kisses onto a man's face and neck and chest. He was lying naked in bed and she was kissing him lovingly and gracefully, her breasts dipping down over him like silvery peonies. Charlotte had never mentioned this to anyone, keeping the picture to herself, a secret snapshot protected from outside sniggerings.

"The loss of romance," bleated the woman, starting afresh.

"We haven't changed," said Harvey stoutly.

"Yes we have! Of course we have!"

"Rubbish."

"But we're *supposed* to change, it's all different now, the baby's got to come first."

"I don't see why," said Harvey. "Mustn't let them rule your life."

The baby had finished at last, and was asleep; the woman gingerly detached her from her body and placed her in the buggy.

"Cheer up," said Harvey, preparing for another dip. "Once you've lost a bit of weight, it'll all be back to normal. Romance et cetera. Get yourself in shape."

"You don't fancy me anymore," she wailed in a last-ditch attempt to hold him.

"No, no, of course I do," he said, eyeing the water. "It's just a bit . . . different from before. Now that you've gone all, you know, sort of floppy."

That did it. At the same moment as the woman unloosed a howl of grief, Nick and Tina released a semi-hysterical screech of laughter. Then—"Run!" said

Joe—and they all shot off round the opposite side of the pool, snatching up their clothes and shoes and purses at the other end. Harvey was meanwhile shouting, "Hoi! Hoi! What the *hell* d'you think you're playing at!" while his wife stopped crying and his daughter started.

The four of them ran like wild deer, leaping low bushes of lavender and thyme, whooping with panicky delight, lean and light and half naked—or, more accurately, nine tenths naked—through the pine trees and *après-midi* dappling. They ran on winged feet, and their laughter looped the air behind them like chains of bubbles in translucent water.

High up on the swimming pool terrace the little family, frozen together for a photographic instant, watched their flight open-mouthed, like the ghosts of summers past; or, indeed, of summers yet to come.

The Door

Organizing a new back door after the break-in was more complicated than you might imagine. Even sourcing a ready-made door to fit the existing frame took some doing. After following a couple of false trails I drove to a little DIY shop five miles away, in a drafty row of shops just off the A3 after the Tolworth Tower turning.

Bleak from the outside, this charmless parade supplied all sorts of seductive and useful items when you looked more closely. Under the dustbin lid of a sky were: a travel agent offering cut-price controlled escapes; a newsagent with a bank of magazine smiles on entry and a surprisingly choice collection of sweets (real Turkish Delight, macadamia praline, Alpine milk chocolate); an art shop with a dusty sleeping cat at the foot of a good wooden easel; a café with Formica tables, a constant frying pan, and a big steel teapot. If you looked closely and in the right way, all the pleasures and comforts were accessible here in this dogleg just off the Tolworth turning, as well as all the nuts and bolts. It was the first time for months that I'd been able to entertain such a thought. In the iron light of February I entered the hardware shop and inside was a little community of goodwill and respect.

The woman on the other side of the counter listened to me attentively, looked at me with kind eyes from behind her glasses, and explained the sizes, finishes, charges, and extras for the various models of ready-made doors they could supply. While she did this she also dealt with a couple of phone calls, politely and efficiently, and paused for a few seconds to admire the baby asleep in the arms of the café owner from next door who had come round with some query about his ceiling, promising herself aloud a cuddle once my order had been taken. Since the seventeenth of August I had grown unimaginative about others, selfishly incurious and sometimes downright hostile. Now, here, some sort of thaw was taking place. A tall man in overalls was talking to the shop's manager, telling him about the progress of a job out in West Molesey, and it seemed it was going well.

There was an atmosphere of good temper that was rare and warming, none of the usual sighs or in-staff carping or reined-in impatience when you wanted to know how much it would be with extra safety bolts or with three coats of paint rather than two. I was charmed. I wanted to stay in this dim toasty light amid the general friendliness and walls festooned with hosepipes, tubes of grouting and sealant, boxes of thumbtacks, lightbulbs, my mind soothed by the industrious but not frantic atmosphere.

Everything here had to do with maintenance and soundness. Grief kept indoors grows noxious, I thought, like a room that can't be aired; mold grows, plants die. I wanted to open the windows but it wasn't allowed.

The order was complicated—did I want full or partial beading; what about a weatherboard; the door furniture, would I prefer a silver or gold finish, or perhaps this brushed aluminium—and it took quite a while. Even so, I was sorry when it was finished and Sally—that was the young woman's name—had handed me my carbon copy and swiped a hundred pounds from my Barclaycard as the deposit. Because even a very ordinary ready-made back door was going to cost £400 in total to supply, fit, hang, and paint.

"They're not cheap, are they, doors," I said, as I signed the slip.

"They're not," Sally sighed in agreement, not taking my comment in any way personally. "But they're well-made, these doors. Nice and strong."

"Good," I said, tucking the Visa slip into my wallet. For a moment I toyed with the idea of telling her how they'd kicked the last one in, but I couldn't face the effort. Even so I felt she was like a sister to me.

"So Matthew will be along on the twenty-second to hang the door and paint it," she said.

"You've got my number in case he needs to change the date."

"Yes, that's right, but expect him on the twenty-second at about nine thirty," she said. "Matthew is very dependable."

At nine thirty-five on the twenty-second I had a phone call, and I relaxed at the sound of Sally's calm voice, even though I was expecting her to cancel the door-fitting appointment with all the irritation that would involve. I had with difficulty arranged a day at home to deal with a couple of files from the office, without having to take it off my annual holiday allowance. But she was not ringing to cancel, no, she was ringing only to let me know that the traffic was terrible that morning and Matthew had rung her to say he was stuck out in a jam near Esher but should be with me before ten.

He arrived at two minutes to, the tall man in overalls I had seen earlier in the shop; he had a frank open face and unforced smile. As he walked into the kitchen at the back my shoulders dropped and I gave a sigh as thorough as a baby's yawn. It was going to be all right.

"Would you like tea or coffee?" I asked, raising the kettle to show this was no idle offer.

"Not just now, thank you," he said. "Later would be good, but I'd better get cracking on straight away."

Again he smiled that nice natural smile. He was not going to be chatty, how wonderful, I would be able to trust him and leave him to it and get on with my work. He did not need respectful hovering attendance as the man who had recently mended the boiler had; nor me running around for step ladders and spare bits and pieces that he might have forgotten, like the electrician before Christmas just after I'd moved in. That had been three months after the funeral I wasn't at. First I'd chucked things out in a sort of frenzy, sackfuls to Oxfam, but then I'd realized that wouldn't be enough, I'd have to move. Which I'd done, somehow.

I hovered around a bit while he brought in his toolboxes. Then, staggering only slightly and with a shallow stertorousness of breathing and blossom of sweat on his forehead, he carried in the door itself, a raw glazed slab of timber that looked too narrow for the destined frame.

"I didn't quite realize . . . ," I said. "I thought it was going to be ready painted, ready to hang today."

"It is ready to hang," he said. "But first I must see how

it fits; I must shave anywhere it's a bit tight. I must see wherever it needs adjusting to the frame."

"Oh, so it's not just standard; I see," I said.

"The frame is a standard size from the measurements you took, but they're always a few millimeters out here and there," he explained. He wasn't irritated or bored by my questions, but at the same time he continued to prepare for work, spreading a groundsheet, setting out his tools.

"We want a perfect fit," he said, looking up, looking me in the eye. "But don't worry, it'll all be done by the end of today."

I hardly ever believe a man when he says that sort of thing, but this one I did. I went into the front room and sat down to work. The disabling sluggishness that had dogged me ever since I'd moved here, stagnant as my reflection in the mirror, seemed to have beaten a temporary retreat. It was more than two hours before I looked up again, though I had been distantly aware of the sounds of drilling and tapping, finding them reassuring rather than distracting. There was satisfaction in two people working separately but companionably in the flat. It was dignified.

I went through to the kitchen.

"Are you ready for a coffee now?" I asked. "It's nearly twelve thirty. I'll be making myself a sandwich, shall I do one for you, too? Just cheese and tomato."

I hadn't cooked anything in this kitchen. Nuts and raisins, toast, that was about it. I really couldn't be bothered.

"I'll say yes to the coffee and no to the sandwich," he said, looking briefly in my direction, his concentration needed for the door, which he appeared to have in a wrestling hold halfway into the frame. "Thank you."

"Can I help?" I said feebly, despising myself immediately for putting him under the necessity of making a polite refusal while struggling with a seven-foot door. The wood was still in its patchy undercoat. Outside, the air was the opposite of crisp, and chill with it.

"Not brilliant painting weather," I commented as I sawed away at the loaf.

"I don't think it'll rain quite yet," he said. "Not till the evening. And the paint should have gone off by then. You'll know when it's gone off, when you're safe, by licking your finger and then just touching the surface of the gloss. If it's smooth, you're safe. If it's still tacky you'll have to wait a bit longer."

Safe—that word—I thought I'd never hear it again. And of course there *is* no safety but it's nice to hear it spoken of.

"Will you really have time to give it two coats?" I said. "What happens after you've applied the first one?"

"Then I have to be a bit patient but it doesn't take as long as you'd think," he said, at work now on lining

17

up the hinges with the places marked for them on the frame.

"Watching paint dry," I suggested, and smiled. I felt better than I had for weeks; I'd worked hard and happily this morning and would continue to do so after my sandwich, with him round the corner. I saw what a ghost I'd become in these rooms, invisible, restless, talking to myself and leaving half-finished sentences in the air.

He had a row of little brass screws held by the line of his lips, like a seamstress with her mouthful of pins, and frowned as he prepared the path for the first of them with the tip of an awl. I put his coffee on the draining board beside him, then perched on a kitchen stool over by the breadbin while I ate my sandwich. The hinges went on well and without trouble. He stood up at last and straightened his back.

"That's more like it," he said, and picked up the mug of coffee.

"It looks lovely," I said truthfully. "The last one was too old, I think, the wood was rotten in the corner and really it wouldn't have kept a squirrel out if it was determined. Let alone a burglar."

"You had a break-in then," he said, shaking his head.

"Opportunistic the police said when they came round," I replied, remembering the two young boys with their notebooks and curt chivalry. One of them had had a large fading bruise on his cheekbone.

"I've got a couple of good sliding bolts to fit on this door," he said. "That and the Chubb lock mean that things should be as secure as they can be."

"Excellent," I said. I wanted to tell him, that meant nothing. Out of the blue your heart can stop beating and you're dead. All finished in twenty minutes. No warning. I'd finished my sandwich. I should go back to the front room table now and make a start on the next file, but somehow I felt like loitering in the kitchen.

"Funny how things come all at the same time," I continued. The business of trying to utter natural words from the heart, frank and clear, struck me with dismal force, the inevitable difficulty involved in discovering ourselves to others; the clichés and blindness and inadvertent misrepresentations; but I thought I would have a go anyway.

"Yes, all sorts of things," I said, but I suddenly couldn't be bothered to mention personal details. One step at a time. One day at a time. Yeah, yeah.

"You just have to put your head down and keep walking, sometimes," I blurted. "Keep on keeping on. Never mind the weather."

He nodded and sipped his coffee. He didn't think I was mad. I *wasn't* mad, but I was very shaken, very shuddery inside when I remembered things. My mind had been behaving like a bonfire: feed it a dry and crackling little worry and it would leap into flame.

"I know what you mean," he said. "When something

happens. Takes over. I've had a few weeks when it's been hard to think of anything else. Well, me and my wife both, really."

He paused, took another sip of coffee.

"These friends of ours," he continued, "a month ago, their flat caught fire, they lived above a garage, it was the wiring, and they lost their two youngest. In the fire. It was in the papers."

"Oh God," I groaned. "How terrible."

My eyes were filling up, my throat had a rock halfway down.

"We've been trying to help see them through it," he said. "But there's not much you can say."

"No," I said.

"You can be there, though," he added, turning back to the door.

"You have to watch it, pity," I said in a rush. "Pity could finish you off."

"That's right," he said. "In the end you have to say to yourself, No, I'm not going to think about that for now. We had to do that, me and my wife, we weren't getting to sleep at night."

"Because it doesn't help anyone in the end," I snorted. "If you go under yourself then you certainly won't be able to hold out a strong hand to help."

"That's right," he said again, and his smile was full of honesty and warmth. I wondered what his wife was like, whether she was equally generous-natured. My dead love had been married, married with a vengeance though he'd never shown me her photo.

"I must get back to my files," I said.

"And I can start on the painting now," he replied, glancing anxiously at the sky.

I had another restorative work session, concentrating well and thoroughly absorbed. Thank God for work. Save us from the obsessive mental mill that constantly grinds but never digests. Secrecy doesn't come naturally to me, and this enforced silence was a punishment for which even his wronged wife might have pitied me, had she known about me. For the first time I wondered what *she* was going through, wherever she was.

Later in the afternoon, Matthew called to me from the kitchen that I should come and have a look.

The door was glossy with its second white coat, immaculate. It had two silver bolts, which he demonstrated would slide easily and slickly into the plates he'd fitted in the frame, and along with the Chubb lock these two would make the door trebly secure. He handed me the small silver key that would fasten them in place, and the larger one for the Chubb, which was gold in color.

"Better not close it for another couple of hours," he suggested. "With luck the rain'll hold off that long; I think it will, but if you shut it before then the paint won't have hardened enough, it'll stick to the frame when you shut it then rip away and leave raw wood when you open it again. So leave it to harden for as long as you can before you shut the door."

I can recognize good advice when I hear it. This was what I'd needed to know.

"Thank you," I said. "Thank you."

The Year's Midnight

Nothing could be more unseasonal than this—the bleachy stench of chlorine, Victorian tiled walls the color of old ivory—and yet, thought Marion as she barreled up the fast lane with flexible body and open chest, perhaps not. It was the winter solstice, December twenty-first, and so she was also aware of swimming in the dark sea of Time with the old year wheeling wearily across the sky above her, the sun very low and weak, and somewhere beneath the horizon the unmarked infant new year waiting its turn.

Moving her whole buoyant body from head to toe in this other element, she took a deep breath and swam a length underwater with goggled eyes open. A desire for immersion is said to signal a longing for a return to the amniotic waters of the womb, a sort of wet version of cozy; but today Marion was looking not for comfort and joy so much as half an hour of daydreaming. Her thoughts were able to roll over weightlessly as she powered along, the centuries revolving back to when (she reflected) men were all fish in Adam's Ale, spermatozoic wrigglers after fusion. It was Saturday afternoon and her husband had taken the girls out Christmas shopping.

The rhythmic movement of the crawl had her blood chiming, and she found herself singing inside her head. Ring out, wild bells, to the wild sky. Adam lay y-bounden. A mere seven hours of light there would be—at most— on this, the shortest day. The year was staggering out on its last legs. As to the bed's-feet life is shrunk; this was the time when very old people decided to give up the ghost. It had been raining for several weeks now, the streets musical with the plash of water cascading from leaking gutters and the busy gurgle of rain streaming down pipes and into drains. People scurried by in moving veils of drizzle, sneezing like burst paper bags.

A serious freeze would be far more welcome; icicles hanging from her nails; like all good swimmers she had long hands and feet. They had looked white as calamari waving there in the inky sea that summer off Lanzarote's volcanic beach. No seafood for her sister, nor much of anything else according to the premonitory voicemail message listing her newly discovered food intolerances—"in fact, nothing but lamb, rice, and pears, the only three foods toward which no one in the history of the world has ever developed an intolerance, extraordinary isn't it?"

And of course we react chemically toward each other as well as to food (mused Marion as she swam on); think of antipathetic siblings slugging it out during childhood and taking care not to meet ever after, or of those unhappy marriages where each has developed a life-threatening allergy to the other. She herself would not tolerate any fallout this Christmas; no, she would hang a mistletoe-decked banner over the front door—BE NICE TO EACH OTHER. Always a recipe for depression, Christmas, when complex adults demanded simple joy without effort, a miraculous feast of stingless memory.

More than half an hour it had been, and with reluctance she hauled her body up into the air and her mind down to earth. It was just gone six, the hinterland of the afternoon, and the changing rooms were almost empty. A tall basket of silver twigs decked with glitter-blobbed baubles stood by the entrance to the showers. There were a few late stragglers in the gated children's area, from which came the sounds of hooting and laughing and crying, and a voice wailing, "I want my daddy." Marion opened her locker and started to peel off her bathing suit.

In the harsh fluorescence of the overhead strip lighting, the bodies of those changing looked frail and faulty. "I hate swimming," she heard one woman say to another,

"I'm doing it for my knee." More design faults, thought Marion; knees, along with ears and teeth, were always causing problems. Doctors and dentists grew fat on them. Buying charity Christmas cards in the local church this year she had been spoiled for choice, wandering from the Multiple Sclerosis Trust to the Stroke Association, then on to Leukemia Research, the Alzheimer's Disease Society, the Parkinson's Disease Society, and Colon Cancer Concern. Roll over a few decades and we'll all be there, she thought, one thing or another will take us all out, each and every one. And that was without the charities that wrestled with cruelty, poverty and war. "Season's Greetings," those cards read; beneath the angel-strain have rolled two thousand years of wrong.

"I want my daddy," howled the child. "I want my daddy I want my DADDY."

"You are being very naughty," came a young voice taut with frustration. "Be quiet! Be quiet!"

Marion and the three other women still there looked up at the scent of danger like antelope pausing on the veldt.

"I want my DADDY I want my DADDY I want my DADDY!"

"Be QUIET. You are not baby! BE QUIET!"

The child started to scream as well as sob and howl. It wired the blood. The woman who had been doing it for her knee looked at her watch and limped briskly off to the exit with her companion. That left Marion, wrapped in a towel and about to have a shower, and another woman who was shaking her head as she pulled up her tights.

This other woman finished changing and went over to the children's area.

"Everything all right?" she asked, putting her head round the corner.

"Is FINE," came the voice over the screaming.

The woman mimed a powerless shrug at Marion, then hurried off out into the rain.

"AAAAH! IWANTMYDADDYIWANTMYDADDY!"

"BE QUIET! You are very naughty girl. You want that I should smack you?"

Not your business, Marion told herself, have your shower. How would *you* have liked it if some nosy woman had come up and criticized you when you were out with Kirsty while she was having one of her tantrums? They used to descend on Kirsty like visitations, fits of hysteria turning her pink and blue and shaking her to the core so that all she, Marion, could do, was wait and hold her until she came down shuddering, storm-shaken, gasping for air. But, she thought, as she held her arms up to the stream of hot water, but . . .

The child's screams continued, ricocheting round the tiles, and rank adrenalin-surging dismay coursed through Marion's veins like some vile drug. I can't stand this, she thought, and knew she'd have to do something. She wrapped a towel round herself before she had time to think, and, dripping, padded over to the source of the screaming.

Within the gated area stood a small girl with scarlet blubbered eyes, sobbing hugely, quite out of control, and a crouching Fury of a young woman who looked up, baleful as Dürer's engraving of Melancholia. There was nobody else left in the changing rooms, only these two in this enclosure, the air around them charged with violence.

Distraction, thought Marion, I must give her something to look at. But she had nothing interesting back in her locker, only her keys, and although a bunch of keys was supposed to have seen John Ruskin through his childhood, times had changed. She looked around her, then unhooked a frosted Santa from the silver twigs at the entrance to the showers.

"Here's Father Christmas!" she declared. She stepped through the gate and handed him to the sobbing child. The noise stopped as though something had been unplugged. This would last for a few seconds only, if memory served her right.

"It's hard," she said, turning to the scowling young woman, and knelt down beside her, uncertainly reaching out and touching her arm. Would she bite?

Beside herself with dark rage, this girl—not much more than a child herself really, at nineteen or twenty—

glared at her but did not after all dare push her away. The peroxide in her hair had reacted badly with the chlorine so that green tinged its yellow; her dark painted eyes raged unhappily in her non-blond face. Here she was, still trying to find herself, still a child exploring her own image, she seemed to say, trapped into fourteen-hour stretches alone with this tiny tyrant. Life was horrible! Life was unfair. Where she came from, it was hard, and here, here she was not free either because she was locked in a daily prison with this screaming lunatic.

Marion patted her arm, then turned to the child, who had started again.

"Now, darling," she said. "There, there. There, there. What pretty beads you're wearing."

The child, puny and fair and hopelessly smudged and blotted and puffy round the eyes, stopped crying for a moment and stood shuddering with sighs, looking back at her uncertainly.

"I've got two girls," said Marion. "They're called Kirsty and Isobel. But they're older than you. They're nine and eleven. And I think you're three. Am I right? Are you three?"

"Yes," nodded the child, gazing at her.

"And let me guess your name," said Marion. "Is it Violet? Is it Amber? Is it Scarlett?"

"No," said the child, shaking her head and giving another long juddery sigh. "It's Lucy."

"What a lovely name," smiled Marion.

She turned to the crouching Fury.

"Everything's going to be fine," she smiled at her.

Her nervous system was on red alert, all the circling horrors roused from five years ago when she was having to invigilate child care for her own two.

"Have you got any brothers or sisters?" she asked Lucy, who looked as though she were about to start again.

"Yes," whispered Lucy. With her fair curling hair she was a Victorian engraver's vision of the New Year. "I've got four brothers. Gabriel and Jack and then sometimes Peter and Michael but some of the times they're in Wakefield. I want my daddy, I want my da . . ."

"I know, and you will see him soon, very soon," soothed Marion. "So, I wonder what presents you will get for Christmas! What a lovely Christmas you will have with all those brothers."

Lucy gave a tremulous smile of assent. At this the baleful girl could contain herself no longer. She gave a great snort, and sneered, "Go with the lady! You don't like ME. That's right, you go with HER."

Lucy's swollen red-rimmed eyes widened.

For pity's sake, thought Marion. Another baby. Don't smash it all up. Your turn now.

"It's very difficult for you," she said carefully, turning to the girl. "Little children . . ."

"She is not baby!" spat the girl. Angry tears oozed from her wild eyes, and long black streaks of salt water and mascara crept down her cheeks.

"I know, I know," soothed Marion. "But in the end they are the children and we are the grown-ups. You understand me? We are not children, we are the grown-ups, and we have to . . ."

"It is not just now," snarled the girl. "She is NAUGHTY. She is like this all the days. All the time she cry, ALL the time."

Marion felt herself shudder. Careful, she told herself. Think of this girl, here, now.

"Where are you from?" she asked.

"Czech Republic," sniffed the girl.

"Will you be going back for Christmas?"

The girl nodded brusquely.

"Well, that will be a holiday," soothed Marion, aware that every minute she spent in phatic chitchat was a minute further from danger. "That will be nice."

"I don't THINK so," said the girl darkly. My family, she implied, is a miserable quarrelsome bunch and things have not improved since our house was caught in the floods and all the carpets and books and clothes ruined. . . . And why it is worse for me than for this horrible child is that I have no MONEY and I have to come here in the rain and dirt to work as a servant in loneliness for people I care nothing about who have too MUCH and my boyfriend is a bastard and I HATE this child, she is very bad with her screaming and crying and nobody knows what I suffer.

"But anyway, whatever happens," said Marion, looking her in the eye, "when you come back in the new year, you must find another job."

"Yes," said the girl. They were both surprised; this was so clearly the right next step to take. It was obvious.

Marion turned back to Lucy, who was still letting out long sighs after her feast of sobbing. Don't touch, she reminded herself, don't hug; she's not yours, you mustn't put your arms round children who don't know you.

"Well, Lucy, everything's going to be all right," she said with the bright simple smile of the fairy on the Christmas tree. This poor youngling for whom we do sing. When she had been upset as a child her grandmother would say to her, It's not worth crying about, we'll all be dead in a hundred years.

"You're going to have a lovely Christmas," she insisted brainlessly in the teeth of the evidence. "You will all be together. And your daddy will say, Here is a lovely present for my best girl Lucy. And everybody will be there, in your family, or they will try to be even if they're a bit late, and when they're all there they will all be *nice* to each other. OK?"

It had got a shade bossy toward the end, she thought, but Lucy's eyes were fixed on her and she had even been tempted into a watery smile. So Marion said it all over again, with extra conviction, and this time it worked even better; as if the more she, Marion, insisted that they would all have a happy Christmas, the more likely it became that they all really would.

Every Third Thought

It happened very fast, without warning. One day everybody started dying. First it was Janey Glazebrook, she woke on a Tuesday in a flood of blood before the school run: bowel cancer. She simply couldn't believe it, she'd had no inkling before except for feeling tired, which, as we all said, let's face it, everybody does. This news, so shocking, was met by talk of Philippa Meekin, Jasmine's mother, who had that very week had an operation to remove a brain tumor. Then Oliver Kitchen was diagnosed with a primary liver tumor and Sadie went to pieces at the school gates—they'd got three under nine and they'd just had the roof taken off for a loft conversion they really couldn't afford so it was utter chaos there. It's like a plague, we all said, an epidemic, a horrible sticky contagion.

"Coincidence," said my husband, Harry, when I told

him the latest over dinner. "These things come in waves, you know, like buses, none for ages then three at the same time." He's some ten years older than me—well, fifteen—so I tried to believe him, as if being older made him more of an expert. I think he married me on the Picasso principle—however old and ugly I get, with any luck I'll still be less old and ugly than him. He's very good at what he does though I couldn't tell you what that is. What I do know is, it takes a lot out of him.

But after all Harry was protected from the bad news by office life. I couldn't even go to Waitrose without bumping into some fresh horror. I'd never had any interest in the subject before, no interest whatsoever. I tend not to dwell on things. Doom and gloom were never my cup of tea, but now they seemed to lurk round every corner.

"Have you heard about Karen Pocock?" said a voice from the other side of the freezer cabinet as I reached in for a packet of organic peas.

"Don't tell me," I blurted, but there was no stopping this bearer of bad news. Stephanie had to be in the thick of it for some reason. She was always the first to know.

Anyway, this time it was Karen Pocock. "Karen Pocock? You *must* know Karen Pocock! She was on the PTA the year they raised enough for a climbing frame, she goes round with that funny expression on her face like there's a bad smell." Karen Pocock, it emerged, had just found out she'd got breast cancer. Six months' chemotherapy ahead of her, no secondaries but two lymph glands involved.

"Yes," said Stephanie, nodding vigorously. "And you'll never believe this but that makes five cases of breast cancer now on Heatherside Avenue."

"Five?"

"Five." Stephanie nodded. "Including Karen's next-door neighbor, can you imagine, she went for tests last week, nothing in her bones but the liver scan seems to show something."

"Five is a lot," I marveled. "Do you think it might be something environmental?"

"What, ley lines?" said Stephanie. "I think not. Myself, I put it down to dairy. And the Pill. Cut out cheese and change to condoms, that's what I say! She had a miscarriage, too, and they say that ups your . . ."

"Must dash," I said, moving away as fast as I could. "See you at the book club. I've got to get Tillie from Tae Kwon Do in a minute."

Harry and I have three girls: Chloe, fourteen, she's a worker, she's started revising for her exams already, a year in advance; Anna, she's eleven, nothing worries her, typical middle child, my little couch potato; and Tillie, who's seven. Tillie was crazed on the Narnia books about then—I associate that time with Mr. Tumnus and Aslan the lion. I remember reading aloud the chapter where

Lucy and Susan watch over Aslan's dead body, and there was a bit where it said, You know that feeling when you've cried yourself to sleep? I can still see Tillie's puzzled round face on the pillow, the way she said, No, Mum, I don't know that feeling. How I beamed with satisfaction at this—smugness, you might call it. Ah well, pride goes before a fall.

It's an odd thing but when someone's been talking to you about breast cancer your own breasts start to fizz and tingle. I wanted to cup mine in my hands right there at the checkout till, and I thought of my girls again. There's a lot of talk now about how it makes sense to go for pre-emptive surgery if you've got a history of breast cancer in the family. You can have both breasts cut off in case and the wounds covered with skin grafts from the back. That would be jumping the gun a bit, Harry said when I mentioned this to him. Still, his grandmother and one of his cousins died of breast cancer. And his aunt.

Adrenalin was in the air. The usual worry, the good old money worry, the mortgage and so on, was pushed to the back in favor of this fertile new health worry. My next-door neighbor told me she now cut out and filed all newspaper columns and magazine articles on cancer—and there are an awful lot of *them*—just in case. "It doesn't do to dwell on things," I said to her. "You could be run over by a bus tomorrow." But my heart wasn't in it; privately

I found myself thinking, That filing business sounds rather a good idea.

"How's Oliver?" I asked Sadie Kitchen the next time I saw her. We were crouched on little wooden chairs waiting in a queue at a parents' evening. It was somewhere in the autumn term, the start of the new school year.

"Not good news," said Sadie with an unhappy grin. "We took him into UCH last night. They said. They said, he probably won't last till November." Her eyes filled. She clenched her face in a horrible helpless smile. I grimaced back and our brimming eyes swam at each other, uselessly.

"They said his tumor's the size of an orange," she said, blowing her nose. "I'd just bought a net of oranges for juicing and they went straight in the bin. I'm not touching oranges again, ever."

I do wish doctors would keep away from food when they're making their comparisons. A prostate gland is the size of a walnut, that sort of thing. Funny what can put you off your food. Tillie wouldn't touch spaghetti after Anna told her it was really dead worms. I used to be crazed on Topic, that chocolate bar with the hazelnuts; I had one on the way back from school every afternoon for years, until there was a court case where a woman bit into one and found a mouse's skull. That completely took the pleasure out of hazelnuts as far as I was concerned.

Somewhere around this time I had to go for a smear.

The practice nurse did it, and once she'd finished digging around and had withdrawn those metal salad servers, I realized how jittery I'd been feeling.

"That didn't hurt a bit," I said as I got dressed. "Thank you." Then I told her about the last few weeks, Death abroad with its scythe, and the state of mind this produced in my circle. If I was looking for reassurance, I was knocking at the wrong door.

"Don't tell me," she said with feeling. She glanced again at my notes. "Ah, you're just the age that starts to happen. I've been there. It was after a party, two in the morning, I found a lump. I was banging on the door first thing in the morning demanding surgery. Nurses are the worst because they see it all the time."

"Yes," I said. "Of course."

"Then suddenly it was happening to so many people. All at once. It's quite a shock. I took out a really good life insurance policy. It makes you decide to enjoy things."

We both looked glum, faced with deserts of vast eternity and the wailing of children left behind.

"The only thing you can do is put your affairs in order," she said, washing her hands vigorously under the tap. "Don't leave too much of a mess."

"But I'm only thirty-six," I said.

She shrugged.

· · ·

After that, for some reason everything I watched on television, every conversation I had with anyone seemed to zoom in on you-know-what. Even the children were interested.

"How old do you want to be when you die?" asked Anna over dinner one night.

"A hundred," said Chloe. "And I want it to happen when I'm asleep."

"A hundred and ten!" said Tillie. "But I want to be awake to see what it's like. As long as it doesn't hurt."

It must have been some time in October, I'd made a recipe from the paper for pumpkin soup, but—like so many pumpkin recipes—it was disappointing, I could tell that from Harry's face. He's very keen on healthy food and no animal fats because of a man at his office having had a heart attack, though I sometimes sneak in a bit of butter for the flavor.

"And would you want to be cremated or buried?" continued Anna.

"That's not very cheerful, darling," I said.

"What's cremated?" asked Tillie.

"Burned in a fire," said Anna, "so there's nothing left except your ashes. Then they put them in a box and give it to your husband to keep under the bed."

"No, your husband scatters the ashes, retard," said Chloe. "Over the sea or from a private jet."

"I don't want to be in the ground if it's like the garden," said Tillie. "I hate worms. But I'm scared of fire."

"Let's change the subject," I said.

"There's this cool new company," said Chloe, looking at me from under her eyelashes. She has beautiful green eyes. She knew she was winding me up. "—this company, which packs your ashes into a giant firework and then you go up into the sky and give a lot of people pleasure at the same time."

"Nang!" said Anna. "I'm choosing that one."

"That's *enough*," said Harry, putting the paper down at last. "Didn't you hear your mother?"

The book group was no better. There was one meeting at Stephanie's house, I remember, which started with her description of Cheyne-Stokes respiration as she poured the wine.

"It comes on just before the end," she cried. "Long gasps of not breathing at all then snorting back in there for a while."

"None for me thanks," I said. "I've put on weight over the summer."

"Ah, but is it *good* fat or *bad* fat?" asked the woman who was holding out the bowl of nuts to me.

"I don't know," I said. "It's about seven pounds."

"Susan's married to an actuary," said Stephanie

proudly. "We were saying the group needed new blood and she's it!"

This introduction was met with a buzz of welcome and interest.

"I used to think actuarial work sounded really boring," said Susan modestly.

Not at all, we assured her; it was *fascinating*. She came under a barrage of excited questions. All I can remember is that it pays to eat sunflower seeds, and that the riskiest decade for tumors starts at the age of forty-five.

"Alan always says that once you reach your fifty-sixth birthday you can breathe again," she laughed, flowering in the sun of our interest.

"Well it certainly starts earlier than that round here," cried Stephanie, filling her glass. "Have you heard the news about Polly Tulloch, girls? She went along to the doctor a bit embarrassed because her wee was looking like beer, very dark, and her pooh had gone white." She paused. We waited. "Turns out she has pancreatic cancer," she concluded, turning down the corners of her mouth like a Greek tragedy mask.

"Who's Polly Tulloch?" I murmured to Juliet, sitting on the sofa beside me.

"I think she does a yoga class with Stephanie," she whispered back, and I was overtaken by a terrible urge to giggle. I pretended to be coughing on some crisps.

"Is it true what my doctor told me?" Juliet pestered the actuary's wife. "That three out of four get it?"

"I heard two in three," added Stephanie.

"Well, but lots of those are over ninety, surely?" said Sally. "A hundred. Then it's just a case of Anno Domino."

"Did anyone read the book?" asked Tricia. "Not to change the subject or anything."

"*Wuthering Heights,*" said Stephanie witheringly. "Didn't do a thing for me."

"Oh no!" cried Tricia. "Didn't you like Heathcliff? I thought Heathcliff was *amazing.*"

"I don't agree," said Stephanie. "Anyway, he dies, for no good reason I could see. What sort of hero's *that*? More wine, anyone?"

But since she'd already told us earlier that our risk of breast cancer rose by 6 percent for every glass we drank, we all said no.

"No, they couldn't get it all out," said Philippa. Her face was steroid-puffy and she'd just been showing me the scar on her partly shaven scalp. She'd kept the staples from her head and held them out to me in a little Murano glass dish.

"It's very aggressive, apparently," she said. "I'm trying to get Greg to see what's happening but he's finding it really hard to, um, take it on board."

I sipped my coffee. I didn't say anything.

"It's difficult for him," said Philippa.

"But it's even more difficult for *you*," I blurted.

"Oh, I don't know," she said casually. "I'm fed up with it. There's been a flood of people I haven't seen for years wanting all the gory details. Stephanie popped by for coffee twice last week, which is as good as having the plague cross painted on your door. I really don't feel up to them."

"I was wondering whether Jasmine and the twins would like an overnight on Friday," I said. "That way they can come trick-or-treating with Tillie."

"Halloween," she shuddered, and flashed me a ghastly grin.

"All Saints," I said feebly.

"I was in Mexico once for the Day of the Dead," she said, closing her eyes. "November first. The family I was staying with took me for a picnic to the graveyard where their relatives were buried and we sat around on tombstones eating little iced sponge cakes baked in the shape of skulls. Keeping them company. Everybody does it there, it had a real party atmosphere."

"You look tired," I said. "Why don't you have a nap? Agnieska's got them till one, hasn't she? How's she working out?"

"I don't know," said Philippa. "There seems to be a lot of screaming and shouting but I can't . . . We've not been

45

an au pair family before. I don't know how to do it. Still, I'm sure I'll learn."

The doorbell rang. It was her next-door neighbor with a batch of flapjacks and a request to cut down some overhanging branches from Philippa's cherry tree.

"Absolutely," said Philippa. "Blocks the light to your kitchen window as it is."

"I must dash," I said. "Got to collect Tillie from her violin lesson."

"I can't think what I want to be most," said Tillie on the way home. "A skellington. Or a witch. No, I don't want to be a witch, all the girls are being witches."

"Jasmine and the twins are coming trick-or-treating with us," I said. "That'll be nice, won't it. I bet they're witches, if they wear the same costumes as last year."

"I might go as a grim reaper," said Tillie.

"Not *a* grim reaper, darling," I corrected her, turning into our road. "*The* grim reaper."

After this, bad news flew in like iron filings to a magnet. One of Anna's teachers went off on compassionate leave when her beautiful student daughter was killed in a car accident. The teenage son of Harry's secretary, Paula, dropped dead of a heart attack during a Sunday morning football match. The woman in the dry cleaner's told me about her husband's seventy-year-old mother who had hung herself from the banisters after her daughter's slow death from cancer.

It was unbearable. I felt wild with fury when I heard such awful things. I thought, That's just not on. It's one thing if you've had a good innings but Philippa *hadn't* had a good innings or anything like it, and neither had most of these people. We'd been led up the garden path. We'd been living in a fool's paradise. I wanted to make a complaint, write a letter to the manager in no uncertain terms.

Stephanie rang to let me know what she'd chosen for the next book club meeting. It was about a man who had been left paralyzed by a stroke but had managed to write his life story by blinking at an amanuensis.

"What a survivor!" said Stephanie admiringly. "Though of course he died. Now, are you going to Oliver Kitchen's funeral on Saturday?"

"I think we might be away," I lied. Harry would be working over the weekend and I didn't want to take Tillie and Anna to a funeral. "Anyway, I don't like it when they say they've just gone into the room next door," I added. "Or that they're having a nice cup of tea with their loved ones in heaven. Sorry, are you religious, Stephanie?"

"I wouldn't say I was *overtly* religious. I mean, I don't feel the need to go to church every Sunday or anything like that." There was a pause, then, "I believe in something to rely on," she said, rather stiffly.

"Yes, that would be nice," I said.

. . .

I suppose I could have gone to the doctor for antidepressants or something to cheer me up, but, well, it struck me that it wasn't *me* that things were the matter with. It was all the rest of it, all these dreadful things happening all over the place. It was the whole setup. *That* was what was the matter. But I did go to the doctor about something else, round about that time.

"When I wake in the night," I told her, "I lie there and I can sometimes feel my heart miss a beat. Quite often."

"Can you describe it a bit more?" she asked, rubbing her eyes and glancing at my notes up on the screen beside her.

"It's like being in a lift and suddenly it plunges down. It's like falling down a liftshaft," I mumbled. I almost added that it felt like a premonition, but stopped myself.

"That sounds perfectly normal," she smiled. "Nothing to worry about, it won't do any harm at all. It's called an extra systole, but really it's nothing to worry about."

"Oh good," I said. "I thought I might need a triple bypass or something."

"There's about as much chance of your needing a triple bypass as of your being run over by a bus," she scoffed. "You could try cutting out coffee, see if that helps. Now, anything else?"

I considered asking about my hot knees, a mysterious

48

new ailment which, according to the medical encyclo-pedia, meant either Lyme disease (though I'd been nowhere near deer) or chlamydia (which would be unlikely at this stage) or—my personal favorite—rheumatoid arthri-tis. But I decided against it.

"No, I'm fine," I said. "Now that I know it's only an extra systole and I'm not just slowly dying."

"Oh we're all doing *that*," she laughed; and so we parted, on a gust of mutual hilarity.

Extra systole or not, I was still having trouble sleeping. That night I gave up and went downstairs, turning on late-night television only to see real-life surgery and the gray-pink gleam of entrails. When I flicked channels the latest brutal massacre leaped onto the screen, as if there wasn't enough carnage around already from natural causes. So I went up to bed again and lay there, full of chewed food, a great useless carcass, a lump of flesh full of lumps of flesh. At five in the morning I woke up shouting, "It's a charnel house!"

"What?" said Harry blearily.

"I'm so *sorry* for everybody," I moaned.

"Worse things happen at sea," grumbled Harry.

"At sea?"

"Go back to *sleep*."

Good cheer and spirits and a smiling face turned to

the sun all looked simply foolish, I decided the next day, sitting at the front of the bus upstairs looking down over a crowded pavement. Childish. Like believing in fairies. Look at all those people. Why weren't they more worried? Particularly the old ones. Why weren't the old ones all tearing round in a panic? Instead they stood there fussing over three pence change.

I was on my way to visit Harry's mother in the Hawthorn Nursing Home, which is on a dual carriageway, making it impossible to park. Hence the bus. When I got there she was sitting feeding peanuts into her cup of tea, traffic whizzing past the window, her wizened silvery arms like birch bark.

"Hello, Eunice," I said. "I've brought you some African violets."

"Do you like beards on men?" she replied.

"No," I said. "I think they hide double chins."

There was a pause and a cold old blue-eyed stare.

"You know it all, don't you?" she said, and smiled in some version of triumph.

Then she started feeding peanuts into her tea again.

"What's the matter?" she said when she saw me staring. "Haven't you seen this done before?"

"Old people," I said to Harry in bed that night. "How do they do it? They just go on and on. Your mother's eighty-seven. And there's Sadie's husband, forty-one, he went running every morning before work and now he's dead."

"It's just the roll of the dice," said Harry, rolling over. "Go to sleep."

"But . . ." I protested.

"You could be run over by a bus," he grunted. "Why not worry about *that*."

Then, about a week later, I *was* run over by a bus. I'd just dropped Tillie off at school and I was on my way back home. I'm glad she wasn't in the car when it happened, it was quite enough of a shock for the girls as it was. Anyway, I was pottering along at about twenty-five thinking about how I ought to stop off at the garden center for some hyacinth bulbs when there was an almighty bang and the next thing I knew I was looking up into a nurse's face and wondering why.

The bus driver had fallen asleep at the wheel; rather extraordinary, that, at nine in the morning. It made the front page of the local paper. The bus had been going downhill, picked up speed, shot a red light, and hit my car broadside on. He'd had a big night out, the driver, and he hadn't bothered going to bed before starting his early-morning shift.

The interesting thing is that, though it was rather awful losing a leg like that, I was back to my old self otherwise. Some sort of cloud lifted and I was out of the woods. Amazing, really. No more doom and gloom! I mean, of *course* there were times when I felt sorry for myself, very sorry for myself, hobbling round in rehab being one of them, but I was always able to snap out of it. It could have been worse. As Harry says, all the important bits are still there.

I've recovered my natural reluctance to dwell on things, thank goodness. You hear people say, "I think about death every day," as if that's something to be proud of, but I can't help thinking, So what? We're none of us going to get any further on that subject until it's our turn. I try not to dwell on how my friend Philippa died because that still makes me cry. It wasn't easy. It was no fun at all. But Karen Pocock got better; I recognized her name when she joined my mosaic class, and now we get on like a house on fire.

Early One Morning

Sometimes they were quiet in the car and sometimes they talked.

"Mum."

"Yes?"

"Can I swear one time in the day? If I don't swear in the others?"

"Why?"

"In the morning. When you come and wake me. Can I say, Bollocks?"

"No."

He's the only person in the world who listens to me and does what I tell him, thought Zoe. That morning when she had gone to wake him he had groaned, unconscious, spontaneous—"Already?" Then he had reached up from his pillow to put strong sleepy arms round her neck.

For these years of her life she was spending more time alone with her boy, side by side in the car, than with anybody else, certainly far more than with her husband, thirty times more, unless you counted the hours asleep. There was the daily business of showing herself to him and to no one else; thinking aloud, urging each other on in the hunt for swimming things, car keys, math books; yawning like cats, as they had to leave soon after seven if they were going to get to school on time. Then they might tell each other the remains of a dream during the first twenty-five minutes on the way to Freda's house, or they might sit in comfortable silence, or sometimes they would talk.

This morning when she had pointed out the sun rising in the east to hit the windscreen and blind them with its flood of flashy light, her nine-year-old boy had scoffed at her and said the earth twizzled on its axis and went round the sun, and how she, his mother, was as bad as the ancient Egyptians, how they sacrificed someone to Ra if the sun went in and finished off everybody when there was an eclipse. It's running out, this hidden time (thought Zoe). You're on your own at eleven, goes the current unwritten transport protocol, but until then you need a minder. Less than two years to go.

"I remember when I was at school," she'd said that morning while they waited for the Caedmon Hill lights. "It seemed to go on forever. Time goes by slowly at school. Slowly. Slowly. Then, after you're about thirty, it goes faster and faster."

"Why?" asked George.

"I don't know," she said. "Maybe it's because after that you somehow know that there'll be a moment for you when there isn't any more."

"Ooh-ah!"

Then he looked at a passing cyclist and commented, "Big arse."

"George!" she said, shocked.

"It just slipped out," he said, apologetic, adult. "You know, like when that man in the white van wouldn't let you in and you said, 'Bastard.' "

Sometimes this daily struggle and inching along through filthy air thick with the thwarted rage of ten thousand drivers gave her, Zoe, pause. It took forty-five minutes to travel the two and three-quarter miles to George's school (Sacred Heart, thanks to his father's faith springing anew, rather than Hereward the Wake half a mile along), and forty-five minutes for her to come back alone in the empty car. In the afternoons it was the same, but the other way round of course, setting off a little after two thirty and arriving back well after four. There was no train. To do the journey by bus, they would have had to catch a 63A then change and wait for a 119 at Sollers Junction. They had tried this, and it had doubled the journey time. Why couldn't there be school buses for everyone as there were in America, the mothers asked one another. Nobody knew why not, but apparently there couldn't. They were just about able to walk it in the same time as it took in the car, and they had tried this, too, carrying rucksacks of homework and packed lunch and sports equipment through the soup of fumes pumped out by crawling cars. Add wind and rain, and the whole idea of pavement travel looked positively quixotic.

"I'll get it, Mum," said George, as her cell phone beeped its receipt of a text.

It was from her friend Amy, whose husband had recently left her for one of his students.

> —If I say anything, he gets very angry [Amy had told her on their last phone call]; he doesn't allow me to be angry.
>
> —But he was the one to leave you.
>
> —Yes. But now he's furious with me, he hates me.
>
> —Do you still love him?
>
> —I don't recognize him. I can't believe this man I ate with and slept beside for fifteen years is capable of being so cold and so, yes, cruel.

Is it true, then, that women can take grief as grief (thought Zoe), but men refuse to do that, they have to convert it into diesel in order to deal with it, all the loss and pain converted into rage?

Her husband had looked around and said, Why don't you do like Sally and Chitra and Mo, organize an au pair, pay for a few driving lessons if necessary, hand it over to someone who'll be glad of the job? She, Zoe, had thought about this, but she'd already been through it all once before, with Joe and Theresa, who were both now at secondary school. She'd done the sums, gone through the interviews in imagination, considered the no-claims bonus; she'd counted the years for which her work time would be cut in half, she'd set off the loss of potential income against the cost of child care, and she'd bitten the bullet. "It's your choice," said Patrick. And it was.

"You're a loser, Mum," her daughter, Theresa, had told her on her return from a recent careers convention. But she wasn't. She'd done it all now—she'd been through the whole process of hanging on to her old self, carving out patches of time, not relinquishing her work, then partly letting go in order to be more with the children, his work taking precedence over hers as generally seemed to be the case when the parents were still together. Unless the woman earned more, which opened up a whole new can of modern worms. Those long-forgotten hours and days were now like nourishing leaf mold round their roots. Let the past go (sang Zoe beneath her breath), time to move on; her own built-in obsolescence could make her feel lively rather than sad. And perhaps the shape of life would be like an hourglass, clear and wide to begin with, narrowing down to the tunnel of the middle years, then flaring wide again before the sands ran out.

"Mum, can you test me on my words?" asked George. He was doing a French taster term, taking it seriously because he wanted to outstrip his friend Mick, who was better than him at math.

"Well, I'm not supposed to," said Zoe. "But we're not moving. Here, put it on my lap and keep your eye open for when the car in front starts to move."

When I was starting out, leaving babies till after thirty was seen as leaving it late (thought Zoe). Over thirty was the time of fade for women, loss of bloom and all that. Now you're expected to be still a girl at forty-two—slim, active, up for it. But if I hadn't done it, had Joe at twenty-six and Theresa at twenty-eight, hammered away at work and sweated blood in pursuit of good childminders, nurseries, au pairs, you name it, and finally, five years later when George came along, slowed down for a while at least, then I wouldn't know why so many women are the way they are. Stymied at some point; silenced somewhere. Stalled. Or, merely delayed?

"It's who, when, where, how, and all that sort of thing," said George. "I'll tell you how I remember *quand*. I think of the Sorcerer's Apprentice because you know he had a WAND, rhymes with *quand,* and then he goes away with all those buckets of water and then WHEN he comes back . . . Get it? WHEN he comes back! That's how it stays in my mind. And *qui* is the KEY in a door and you answer it and who is there? WHO! I thought of all that myself, yeah. Course. And *ou* is monkeys in the rainforest. Oo oo oo. Hey look, it's moving."

They crawled forward, even getting into second gear for a few seconds, then settled again into stasis.

"Why the rainforest?" asked Zoe. "Monkeys in the rainforest?"

"Because, WHERE are they?" he asked. "Where *are* they, the trees in the rainforest. That's what the monkeys want to know, oo oo oo. Cos they aren't there anymore, the trees in the rainforest."

"You remember everything they teach you at school, don't you?" said Zoe admiringly.

"Just about," said George with a pleased smile. "Mum, I don't want you to die until I'm grown up."

There was a pause.

"But I don't want to die *before* you," he added.

"No, I don't want that either," said Zoe.

This boy remembers every detail of every unremarkable day (thought Zoe), he's not been alive that long and he's got acres of lovely empty space in his memory bank. Whereas I've been alive for ages and it's got to the point where my mind is saying it already has enough on its shelves, it just can't be bothered to store something new unless it's *really* worth remembering.

I climb the stairs and forget what I'm looking for. I forgot to pick up Natasha last week when I'd promised her mother, and I had to do a three-point turn in the middle of Ivanhoe Avenue and go back for her and just hope that none of the children already in the car would snitch on me. But that's nothing new. I can't remember a thing about the last decade or so, she told other mothers, and they agreed, it was a blur, a blank, they had photographs to prove it had happened but they couldn't remember it themselves. She, Zoe, saw her memory banks as having shriveled for lack of sleep's welcome rain; she brooded over the return of those refreshing showers and the rehydration of her pot-noodle bundles of memories, and how (one day) the past would plump into action, swelling with import, newly alive. When she was old and free and in her second adolescence, she would sleep in royally, till midday or one. Yet old people cannot revisit that country, they report; they wake and listen to the dawn chorus after four or five threadbare hours, and long for the old three-ply youth-giving slumber.

They had reached Freda's house, and Zoe stopped the car to let George out. He went off to ring the bell and wait while Freda and also Harry, who was in on this lift, gathered their bags and shoes and coats. It was too narrow a road to hover in, or rather Zoe did not have the nerve to make other people queue behind her while she waited for her passengers to arrive. This morning she shoehorned the car into a minute space three hundred yards away, proudly parking on a sixpence.

What's truly radical now though (thought Zoe, rereading the text from Amy as she waited) is to imagine a man and woman having children and living happily together, justice and love prevailing, self-respect on both sides, each making sure the other flourishes as well as the children. The windscreen blurred as it started to rain. If not constantly, she modified, then taking turns. Where *are* they?

But this wave of divorces (she thought), the couples who'd had ten or fifteen years or more of being together, her feeling was that often it wasn't as corny as it seemed to be in Amy's case—being left for youth. When she, Zoe, looked closely, it was more to do with the mercurial resentment quotient present in every marriage having risen to the top of the thermometer. It was more to do with how the marriage had turned out, now it was this far down the line. Was one of the couple thriving and satisfied, with the other restless or foundering? Or perhaps the years had spawned a marital Black Dog, where one of them dragged the other down with endless gloom or bad temper or censoriousness and refused to be comforted, ever, and also held the other responsible for their misery.

There had been a scattering of bust-ups during the first two or three years of having babies, and then things seemed to settle down. This was the second wave, a decade or so on, a wild tsunami of divorce as children reached adolescence and parents left youth behind. The third big wave was set to come when the children left home. She, Zoe, had grown familiar with the process simply by listening. First came the shock, the vulnerability and hurt; then the nastiness (particularly about money) with accompanying baffled incredulity; down on to indignation at the exposure of unsuspected talents for treachery, secretiveness, two-faced liardom; falling last of all into scalding grief or adamantine hatred. Only last week her next-door neighbor, forced to put the house on the market, had hissed at her over the fence, "I hope he gets cancer and dies." Though when it came to showing round prospective purchasers, the estate agents always murmured the word "amicable" as reassurance; purchasers wanted to hear it was amicable rather than that other divorce word, *acrimonious*.

She peered into the rearview mirror and saw them trudging toward her with their usual heaps of school luggage. It was still well before eight and, judging herself more bleached and craggy than usual, she added some color just as they got to the car.

"Lipstick, hey," said George, taking the front seat. The other two shuffled themselves and their bags into the back.

"I used to wear makeup," said Zoe. "Well, a bit. When I was younger. I really enjoyed it."

"Why don't you now?" asked Freda. Freda's mother did, of course. Her mother was thirty-eight rather than forty-two. It made a difference, this slide over to the other side, reflected Zoe, and also one was tireder.

"Well, I still do if I feel like it," she said, starting the car and signaling. She waited for a removal van to lumber along and shave past. "But I don't do it every day like brushing my teeth. It's just another thing." Also, nobody but you lot is going to see me so why would I, she added silently, churlishly.

She was aware of the children thinking, What? *Why* not? Women *should* wear makeup. Freda in particular would be on the side of glamour and looking one's best at all times.

"We had a Mexican student staying with us once," she told them, edging onto the main road. "And at first she would spend ages looking after her long glossy hair, and more ages brushing makeup onto her eyelids and applying that gorgeous glassy lip gloss. But after a while she stopped, and she looked just like the rest of us—she said to me, it was a lovely holiday after Mexico City, where she really couldn't go outside without the full works or everybody would stare at her. So she kept it for parties or times when she felt like putting it on, after that."

"Women look better with makeup," commented Harry from the back. Harry's au pair dropped him off at Freda's on Tuesday and Thursday mornings, and in the spirit of hawk-eyed reciprocity on which the whole fragile school-run ecosystem was founded, Zoe collected George

from Harry's house on Monday and Wednesday afternoons, which cut *that* journey in half.

"Well, I'm always going to wear makeup when I'm
older," said Freda.

"Women used to set their alarm clocks an hour early so
they could put on their false eyelashes and lid liner and
all that," said Zoe. "Imagine being frightened of your husband seeing your bare face!"

There was silence as they considered this; grudging
assent, even. But the old advice was still doing the
rounds, Zoe had noticed, for women to listen admiringly
to men and not to laugh at them if they wanted to snare
one of their very own. Give a man respect for being higher
caste than you, freer, more powerful. And men, what was
it men wanted? Was it true they wanted only a cipher?
That a woman should not expect admiration from a man
for any other qualities than physical beauty or selflessness? Surely not. If this were the case, why live with such
a poor sap if you could scrape your own living?

"Do you like Alex?" asked Harry. "I don't. I hate Alex,
he whines and he's mean and he cries and he whinges all
the time. But I pretend I like him, because I want him to
like me."

There was no comment from the other three. They
were sunk in early-morning torpor, staring at the static
traffic around them.

"I despite him," said Harry.

"You can't say that," said Freda. "It's *despise*."

"That's what I said," said Harry.

George snorted.

It was nothing short of dangerous and misguided (thought Zoe) not to keep earning, even if it wasn't very much and you were doing all the domestic and emotional work as well, for the sake of keeping the marital Black Dog at bay. Otherwise if you spoke up it would be like biting the hand that fed you. Yes, you wanted to be around (thought Zoe), to be an armoire, to make them safe as houses. But surrendering your autonomy for too long, subsumption without promise of future release, those weren't good for the health.

"I hate that feeling in the playground when I've bullied someone and then they start crying," said Harry with candor.

"I don't like it if someone cries because of something I've said," said Freda.

"I don't like it when there's a group of people and they're making someone cry," said George over his shoulder. "That makes me feel bad."

"Oh, I don't mind that," said Harry. "If it wasn't me that made them cry. If it was other people, that's nothing to do with me."

"No, but don't you feel bad when you see one person like that," replied George, "and everyone picking on them, if you don't, like, say something?"

"No," said Harry. "I don't care. As long as *I'm* not being nasty to them I don't feel bad at what's happening."

"Oh," said George, considering. "I do."

"Look at that car's number plate," said Freda. "The letters say XAN. XAN! XAN!"

"FWMMM!" joined in Harry. "FWMMFWMM! FWMM FWMMFWMM!"

"BGA," growled George. "BGA. Can you touch your nose with your tongue?"

Zoe stared out from the static car at the line of people waiting in the rain at a bus stop, and studied their faces. Time sinks into flesh (she mused), gradually sinks it. A look of distant bruising arrives, and also for some reason asymmetry. One eye sits higher than the other and the mouth looks crooked. We start to resemble cartoons or caricatures of ourselves. On cold days like today the effect can be quite trollish.

"Who would you choose to push off a cliff or send to prison or give a big hug?" George threw over his shoulder. "Out of three—Peter Vallings—"

"Ugh, not Peter Vallings!" shrieked Freda in an ecstasy of disgust.

"Mrs. Campbell. And—Mr. Starling!"

"Mr. Starling! Oh my God, Mr. Starling," said Harry, caught between spasms of distaste and delight. "Yesterday he was wearing this top, yeah, he lets you see how many ripples he's got."

Your skin won't stay with your flesh as it used to (thought Zoe), it won't move and follow muscle the way it did before. You turn, and there is a fan of creases however trim you are; yet once you were one of these young things at the bus stop, these over-eleven secondary school pupils. Why do we smile at adolescent boys, so unfinished, so lumpy (she wondered) but feel disturbed by this early beauty of the girls, who gleam with benefit, their hair smooth as glass or in rich ringlets, smiling big smiles and speaking up and nobody these days saying, "Who do you think you are?" or "You look like a prostitute." It's not as if the boys won't catch up with a vengeance.

"I love my dog," said Harry fiercely.

"Yes, he's a nice dog," agreed Freda.

"I love my dog so much," continued Harry, "I would rather die than see my dog die."

"*You* would rather die than your *dog?*" said George in disbelief.

"Yes! I love my dog! Don't you love *your* dog?"

"Yes. But . . ."

"You don't really love your dog. If you wouldn't die instead of him."

Zoe bit her tongue. Her rule was, never join in. That way they could pretend she wasn't there. The sort of internal monologue she enjoyed these days came from being round older children, at their disposal but silent.

67

She was able to dip in and out of her thoughts now with the freedom of a bird. Whereas it was true enough that no thought could take wing round the under-fives; what they needed was too constant and minute and demanding, you had to be out of the room in order to think and they needed you *in* the room.

When George walked beside her he liked to hold on to what he called her elbow flab. He pinched it till it held a separate shape. He was going to be tall. As high as my heart, she used to say last year, but he had grown since then; he came up to her shoulder now, this nine-year-old.

"Teenagers!" he'd said to her not long ago. "When I turn thirteen I'll be horrible in one night. Covered in spots and rude to you and not talking. Jus' grunting."

Where did he get all that from? The most difficult age for girls was fourteen, they now claimed, the parenting experts; while for boys it was nineteen. Ten more years then. Good.

"Would you like to be tall?" she'd asked him that time.

"Not very," he'd said decisively. "But I wouldn't like just to be five eight or something. I'd want to be taller than my wife."

His *wife*! Some way down the corridor of the years, she saw his wife against the fading sun, her face in shade. Would his wife mind if she, Zoe, hugged him when they met? She might, she might well. More than the father giving away his daughter, the mother must hand over her son. Perhaps his *wife* would allow them only to shake hands. When he was little his hands had been like velvet, without knuckles or veins; he used to put his small warm hands up her cardigan sleeves when he was wheedling for something.

They were inching their way down Mordred Hill, some sort of delay having been caused by a juggernaut trying to back into an eighteenth-century alley centimeters too narrow for it. Zoe sighed with disbelief, then practiced her deep breathing. Nothing you could do about it, no point in road rage, the country was stuffed to the gills with cars and that was all there was to it. She had taken the Civil Service exams after college and one of the questions had been, How would you arrange the transport system of this country? At the time, being utterly wrapped up in cliometrics and dendrochronology, she had been quite unable to answer; but now, a couple of decades down the line, she felt fully qualified to write several thousand impassioned words, if not a thesis, on the subject.

But then if you believe in wives and steadfastness and heroic monogamy (thought Zoe, as the truck cleared the space and the traffic began to flow again), how can you admit change? Her sister Valerie had described how she was making her husband read aloud each night in bed from *How to Rescue a Relationship*. When he protested, she pointed out that it was instead of going to a marriage guidance counselor. Whoever wants to live must forget, Valerie had told her drily; that was the gist of it. She, Zoe, wasn't sure that she would be able to take marriage guidance counseling seriously either, as she suspected it was probably done mainly by women who were no longer needed on the school run. It all seemed to be about women needed and wanted, then not needed and not wanted. She moved off in second gear.

No wonder there were gaggles of mothers sitting over milky lattes all over the place from 8:40 a.m. They were recovering from driving exclusively in the first two gears for the last hour; they had met the school deadline and now wanted some pleasure on the return run. Zoe preferred her own company at this time of the morning, and also did not relish the conversation of such groups, which tended to be fault-finding sessions on how Miss Scantlebury taught long division or postmortems on reported classroom injustices, bubblings-up of indignation and the urge to interfere, still to be the main moving force in their children's day. She needed a coffee though—a double macchiato, to be precise—and she liked the café sensation of being alone but in company, surrounded by tables of huddled intimacies each hived off from the other, scraps of conversation drifting in the air. Yesterday, she remembered, there had been those two women in baggy velour tracksuits at the table nearest to her, very solemn.

"I feel rather protective toward him. The girls are very provocative the way they dress now. He's thirteen."

"Especially when you're surrounded by all these images. Everywhere you go."

"It's not a very nice culture."

"No, it's not."

And all around there had been that steady self-justificatory hum of women telling one another the latest version of themselves, their lives, punctuated with the occasional righteous cry as yet another patch of moral high ground was claimed. That's a real weakness (she thought, shaking her head), and an enemy of, of— whatever it is we're after. Amity, would you call it?

"Last year when we were in Cornwall we went out in a boat and we saw sharks," said Harry.

"Sharks!" scoffed George. "Ho yes. In *Cornwall*."

"No, really," insisted Harry.

"It's eels as well," said Freda. "I don't like them either."

"Ooh no," Harry agreed, shuddering.

"What about sea snakes?" said George. "They can swim into any hole in your body."

The car fell silent as they absorbed this information.

"Where did you hear this?" asked Zoe suspiciously; she had her own reservations about Mr. Starling.

"Mr. Starling told us," smirked George. "If it goes in at your ear, you're dead because it sneaks into your brain. But if it goes up your . . ."

"What happens if it gets in up there?" asked Harry.

"If it gets in there, up inside you," said George, "you don't die but they have to take you to the hospital and cut you open and pull it out."

The talk progressed naturally from here to tapeworms.

"They hang on to you by hooks all the way down," said Harry. "You have to poison them, by giving the person enough to kill the worm but not them. Then the worm dies and the hooks get loose and the worm comes out. Either of your bottom or somehow they pull it through your mouth."

"That's enough of that," said Zoe at last. "It's too early in the morning."

They reached the road where the school was with five minutes to spare, and Zoe drew in to the curb some way off while they decanted their bags and shoes and morning selves. Would George kiss her? She got a kiss when they arrived only if none of the boys in his class was around. He knew she wanted a kiss, and gave her a warning look. No, there was Sean McIlroy; no chance today.

They were gone. The car was suddenly empty, she sat unkissed, redundant, cast off like an old boot. Boohoo, she murmured, her eyes blurring for a moment, and carefully adjusted her side mirror for something to do.

Then George reappeared, tapping at the window, looking stern and furtive.

"I said I'd forgotten my math book," he muttered when she opened the car door, and, leaning across as though to pick up something from the seat beside her, smudged her cheek with a hurried—but (thought Zoe) unsurpassable—kiss.

The Tree

"I'm very worried," she said. "Can you come over right away, Derek?"

"Listen, Mum," I said through gritted teeth, "I'm on my cell phone. I'm sitting in a traffic jam in Chudleigh Road. Is it urgent?"

"It's that dead tree in the back garden," she said. "I'm really worried about it. It's a danger to life and limb."

"Do you know where Chudleigh Road is, Mum?" I said. "It's in between Catford Greyhound Stadium and Ladywell Cemetery. And you're over in Balham."

"Never mind that," she said. Then, "Ladywell used to be a lovely area. Very what-what."

"Well it isn't anymore," I snapped, glaring out of the car window into the November drizzle.

"I'm really worried, Derek," she said. "That tree out the back, it's dead and now the wall beside it is shaky and it might fall on someone."

"That wall is only shaky because you went and got rid of the ivy," I told her, crawling along in first, trying not to sound irritated.

"Ivy is a weed," she said with surprising force.

I hate ivy too. It makes me shudder. To me it's the shade-loving plant you find in graveyards feeding off the dead.

"You should have left it alone," I said. "It was helping hold that wall up. Parasitical symbiosis."

When I was over in Balham two days ago she took me to look at the tree, which was definitely dead and was at that point covered in strangulating ivy. There were flies and wasps crawling all over the ivy berries when you looked, and also snails lurking under the dark green leaves that smothered the wall.

"I did a good job getting rid of it," she said down the phone. "I ripped it all out, it took me the full morning."

Her memory may not be what it was but physically she's still quite strong. I could just imagine the state of the old brickwork after she'd torn away the ivy, the dust and crumbling mortar. No wonder the wall was shaky after that.

"You should have left it to me," I said tetchily. "I'd have cut the stems and left it a few weeks. That way all those little aerial roots would have shriveled up a bit and lost their grip on the brickwork. It would have come away easily if you'd only left it a bit."

There was a pause, then I heard her start up again.

"I'm really worried, Derek. It's that dead tree in the back garden. Can you come over?"

"Listen, Mum," I said, and my voice was a bit louder than I meant. "You keep saying the same thing. I heard you the first time, you know. You're repeating yourself, over and over again, did you know that?"

"Oh dear," came her voice after another pause. "I suppose it's true. You've said so before and you wouldn't make it up."

"Don't worry," I said, immediately remorseful. "It's not the end of the world. Me, I'm forgetting names all the time now that I've reached fifty."

"Are you fifty?" she said, and she sounded quite shocked.

I wasn't making it up about the memory. I go hunting for a word, searching up and down my brain, and just as I think I've got it, it's gone—like a bird flying out the window.

"It's important to forget things," I said down the phone. "We've got too much to remember these days."

"It's a bit worrying though, isn't it," she said.

"Well, you can just stop worrying," I said, seeing the traffic start to move at last. "Stop worrying about that tree. I can't come now, I've got too much work on my plate, but I'll be over on Saturday. Okay?"

I had so much work on that it wasn't funny. I was on my way back to the office in New Cross, where there was a pile of stuff to be dealt with, then I had to be over at the house in Bassano Street by three, which would be cutting it fine but I'd have a sandwich in the van on the way. I was going to go round it with Paul, the surveyor, before starting in on the structural stuff, just for a second opinion. We put business each other's way on a regular basis, so it works quite well.

Now a surveyor really *does* have to worry. That's what he's there for, to worry. He worries for a living. It's up to him to spy the hairline crack in the wall that will lead to underpinning in five years' time. See that damp patch? That's hiding wet rot, which in turn leads to dry rot, and dry rot will spread through a house like cancer. You have to cut the brickwork out if it gets bad enough.

Seeing a house for the first time, you can tell everything about it that you need to know if your eyes are open. It's the same between men and women, the first meeting. You know everything on the first meeting alone, if you're properly awake. And as things go on, it'll be the first cold look, the first small cruelty that lays bare the structural flaws.

Martine would never even consider having my mother to live with us. "I am not marrying you so that I can be a tower of strength and a refuge to your relatives," she said. I drop by when I'm passing through Balham, generally once or twice a week, and I tend not to mention it to Martine when I do so. "I have the right to decline responsibility for other people's problems," says Martine, and I agree with her. She is the first woman in my life who doesn't lean or cling, and this is a luxury I had not thought possible. She's independent yet she chooses to be with me. I can hardly believe it. Anyway, I left Vicky and the boys for her. I can't talk about selfishness.

Later I had to ring Paul to say I was running late for Bassano Street. I had to track him down on his cell phone in the end because he was already there. He started telling me about the dodgy flaunching on the chimney stacks, but far more interesting than that was the news on the Choumert Road house I'd sent him to check out that morning.

"I went down into the cellar and I couldn't believe my eyes," he said, sounding quite excited for him. "Asbestos everywhere. I've never needed my mask before in all my years in this job and of course I couldn't find it when I needed it so I had to make do with a piece of paper towel . . ."

"You're going a bit over the top, aren't you?" I said, because I'd liked the look of that house. "Can't you just case it in and seal it off?"

"Normally I'd say yes," came his voice. "But this stuff

was crumbling, it was in a dreadful condition. White dust everywhere."

"Even so," I said, not wanting to give up on the house, which had looked a nice safe bet to me when I'd seen it the week before.

"More people die of asbestosis every year than die in road accidents," he said. "Did you know that? You don't get to hear about it because it's mainly building workers who get it. Like my father."

"Okay," I said. "Message received."

Funny how the picture of a safe solid-looking house can cave in on itself to reveal a rotting deathtrap, all in a few seconds.

The next day my mother rang me again, and this time I was at the office battling with the VAT returns. She was in a real state, very upset, sounding guilty and at the same time humiliated. It was that tree again, of course.

Gradually I got the story out of her, how she couldn't wait, she'd been so worried about the tree that she couldn't think about anything else, so right after my last call she'd dug out a copy of the Yellow Pages and got some tree specialists along.

"You think I'm incapable," she said at this point in the story. "You think I can't do anything on my own anymore."

When the men arrived, she told them, "I only have

eight hundred and twenty-five pounds in my savings account. Will that be enough?"

"That should do it," they assured her, and I can just imagine them struggling to keep their ugly faces straight.

So she left the three men in her house, alone, while she went down to the Abbey National to draw out her entire savings. When she got back she watched them cut the tree down, which took about five minutes. They cleared some of the rubbish, pocketed her money, and said they'd be back to deal with the roots. She hadn't seen them since.

"They promised they'd be back right away with some poison for the roots," she said, and she was almost in tears. "They haven't finished the job. The roots are the most important bit, aren't they, Derek."

Of course, I knew it could have been a lot worse. Stories centring round the vulnerability of old ladies, they're what keep the *South London Press* in business, as you'd know if you read that paper. New mothers are notorious for going to pieces over sad news items involving children, and in just the same way I am overcome by tales of helpless elderly women like my mother being robbed blind or beaten up or worse.

I realize Martine might seem hard to some people, but she's just frightened of getting old. Before bed she always rubs handcream into her elbows and her upper arms as well as into her hands. She knows how to look after herself. My mother is not like that. Her hands are mine, so is the way she holds herself and the line of her worried brow. She has trouble with her hips, her shoulders, and so do I. She is losing her memory. So will I. There's a phrase I have to describe her to myself. I saw it in one of those poems they stick up now on the Underground along with the adverts. When I read the words, I thought, that's her: Ancient Person of My Heart.

"Am I talking sense, Derek?" she said last time I visited. I said of course she was. She went round the houses sometimes, I said; but that was allowed once you were no spring chicken.

One day she'll look at me and she won't remember me. She won't know anything about me, who I am or what I'm called or the baby I once was in her arms. It happened to her own mother after all, and I daresay it will happen to me. My grandmother's last ten years were spent in a bad dream of not knowing who or where she was, until she fell off the edge at last into the final darkness.

"What's the number, Mum?" I said down the phone, and I kept on at her until I had it. She was sure she'd lost it but then I told her to go and fetch the Yellow Pages and when she came back to the phone with it there, sure enough, she had circled their name and number in ball point pen.

"Right," I said, taking down the number. "Leave this to me, Mum. And you stop worrying, do you hear me."

I dialed and waited, then demanded to speak to the manager. I was reasonably under control at this point, I'm sure I was, but there must have been something in my voice because the man whistled and said, "Who are *you*." Very calm and controlled, I told him how my elderly mother had had his men in to deal with a dead tree in her garden; how I was concerned about the extortionate fee they'd charged her; how they'd not been back as promised to remove the rubbish; and how they hadn't even finished the job. "What's the point of cutting down the tree and leaving the roots?" I demanded, my voice rising. "The roots need to be poisoned and then, later, dug up. Call yourself tree surgeons?"

He listened to my story in silence. He heard me out. Then he flatly denied his men had ever been there.

Of course, I thought. Bastard. I banged the phone down and I was shaking. I sat there and I began to boil with rage. I started to think through what I would like to do to them, that bunch of crooks. Smash their windows. Their legs. Then I had an idea. I leafed through my address book and punched in the number of a debt-collector friend of mine. I gave him the story, gave him their address and number. I told him to get the money back whatever way he liked, and he could have half.

When I am old and have the illness my mother is now entering, I will remember this while the rest is slipping away. And Martine no doubt will have come to a just estimate of the situation and of her own needs, and will have arranged suitable care for me. As I will have to, eventually, for my mother. For I cannot look after her indefinitely, I cannot wander away there with her, hand in hand.

I rang the tree crooks back and went completely ballistic. I threatened them with the strong arm of the law and with all sorts of illegal strong-arm stuff, too. I moralized at them and told them what scum they were, what vermin, taking advantage of a defenseless widow; how they deserved to rot in hell. I poured a molten screaming lava of vileness into the mouthpiece and then I slammed the phone down.

The noise I'd been making, I must have brought the rest of the office to a standstill. I was completely shaken up, shuddering with indignation. I was exhausted. Plus I had three appointments lined up that afternoon for which I was now running late.

Someone slid a mug of coffee onto my desk, with a message to ring my mother. I took a few slow deep breaths. I took a sip of the coffee. Then I rang her back.

She told me she was very sorry but she'd given me the wrong number. She hoped she hadn't caused any trouble. After giving me that number she'd circled in the Yellow Pages, she'd wandered off and found a business card on her hall table. It belonged to another firm of tree surgeons altogether, and this lot were definitely the ones who'd been round and done the work. She remembered them leaving the card on the hall table, she remembered them pointing it out to her. She'd tried to ring me back about it right away, but I'd been engaged.

Since that business with the tree, she's been on the blower to me about every little thing. She's totally lost confidence in her own judgment. She rings me at the office, and also at home, which she never used to do. Martine is fast losing patience. She rings me up to ask my advice over every tiny detail. A man has offered to clean her windows for ten pounds—is that too much? Every little thing. It's driving me mad.

In the Driver's Seat

I was crouched in the back of Deborah's car. Her bluff new boyfriend was driving it, rather brutally, down the A4 in the dark through the rain. We were on our way to Maidenhead, where the party was. He knew the road well so he was driving with a sort of braggartly contempt.

"I had no idea your car could get up this sort of speed, Deborah," I said.

"It's not a *new* car," said Deborah with a nervous laugh.

"She can tell *that,*" scoffed Andy. "It's shaking so much it feels like it'll fall to bits."

"Perhaps it's not used to . . . ," said Deborah, and I saw her hand grip the dashboard, which goaded Andy into putting his foot down even further.

He belted us along with breezy boyishness, although he is now thirty-six. He looks like what he is, a former rugby player. Injuries stopped him a couple of years ago and he's concerned about running to fat.

"You should try rowing now you're living in Isleworth," I had said over dinner. "You really should, you're the right build; you'd love it."

I noticed how he bristled, how a sullen flash of resentment flew at me from his forcefield.

"Andy doesn't like being told what he'd like," laughed Deborah watchfully across the table.

Back on the A4 Andy was intent on forcing the car, a decent elderly Polo, up into the nineties if he possibly could. Deborah was at the limit of her tact and patience.

"I'm not sure my poor old car will be able to take this," she murmured.

"You'll never know till you try!" caroled Andy above the roaring of the engine.

"Actually I'm feeling a bit sick," she said, uncertain, but it made no difference.

He obviously couldn't bear to be in the passenger seat unless it was absolutely necessary—that is, unless he'd had what he would call a skinful. The way a man drives gives a surprisingly accurate idea of what he's like in other areas. Does he crash his way through the gears? Does he speed, or stall? Does he get nasty at the lights? I gazed at the back of Andy's head. You certainly wouldn't want *him* sitting on your tail, I thought, with a coarse mental chuckle.

I was trying to disregard the awareness that I was bumping along on a mad dangerous out-of-control toboggan ride. It seemed a good time to describe my next-door neighbor's teenage daughter's horror when I'd told her how the new speed cameras work. Her eyes had stretched in shock. She'd obviously been speeding all over London in her father's Ford Mondeo, I said. They photograph the face at the wheel as well as the car's number plates, I'd told her. Deborah skipped the laugh in the story and went straight for the element that worried her.

"The thing is, Andy," she said, would-be brave, trying to sound mock-truculent, "this *is* my car and if it's photographed by the speed cameras, I'll be the one who's held responsible."

"Hohoho!" said Andy, spitefully, I thought.

"I'm not joking anymore, Andy," she said, still timid in the shade of his massive macho aura. "I could lose my license."

"Oh dear me!" crowed Andy, and the car bowled creakingly along at ninety.

Was he wanting her to beg him?

"But then I'd find it very difficult to keep my job," she protested. "It's not funny."

"No, it's *not* funny," he mocked, not slackening the pace at all.

She is five years older than him, gets back from work in time to help her two children with their homework, reviews the rate she pays on her mortgage every half year. She is beautiful in the sepulchral Victorian manner, her expression veering between anxiety and seriousness; whereas he plays the fool, the tease, the cossetted grasshopper to her credit-worthy ant.

"Yes, he's living in my house now but he doesn't contribute to the bills or food," she confided in me over coffee. "Whenever we go out together, I have to drive us home because he likes to drink. He never buys a present when we visit my friends or family, that's always up to me."

"Tell him how you feel," I said. Presumably she didn't want me to come over breathless with indignation on her behalf. She didn't need *me* to state the bleeding obvious, she could see that for herself.

"Well, I do; I have to say what I think," she continued. "But it makes me feel I'm mercenary, these uncomfortable feelings. Because he's lovely really. And I like being with someone. I've been on my own for a while now and everything's fine, my job's secure, the children are fine; but I want to be married again, that's the trouble, I like the married state. And Andy wants to belong. He wants to get married, he said to me, 'What if anything were to happen to you? I wouldn't feel secure unless I knew I could stay on in the house.' And of course there's always the fear that he might leave me. He would feel happier if I transferred the house title into joint names. Men like to be trusted, don't they?"

"I imagine we all do," I'd said. "Like to be trusted."

"I'll be forty-one next year. Andy's saying he wants my child!" She laughed, hand swiping her brow, and looked down at the table in confusion.

That had been some weeks ago. The rain was very heavy now, the windscreen wipers were going at a double lick. Why on earth had I agreed to a lift to this party? I thought of my own car, my little green Fiat, with longing. I love my car. It makes me feel light and free. It means nobody can bully me about not drinking and I can leave whenever I want to. All those sulky end-of-party dramas of coercion and constraint, the driver wanting to go and the drinker wanting to stay, I don't have to do them; although I would tonight. Why had I said yes?

I looked at the two antagonistic heads in front of me, his and hers, parental, and I felt like a child crouching in the back on my own. Their child.

"Andy, I really am feeling a bit sick," said Deborah faintly. "I do wish you'd slow down."

That brought back Deborah's troubled laughter over coffee that time, her hand swiping her brow in confusion as she told me what he wanted. And I thought—I *wonder*.

If I'm Spared

"What are you wearing," he muttered into his cell phone, noncommittal.

She told him, in detail, and while he listened he drew down deep drafts of nicotine and narrowed his eyes. She had a small hard waist, Fiona, and was proud of what in Pilates-speak was described as her inner corset.

"Are you coming in?" called Barbara, plaintive, from the back door. "It's gone ten."

"In a minute," he replied.

"Tom . . ."

"I said, in a minute."

The row of tall terraced houses in which he lived backed onto the little gardens of another row of tall terraced houses. Many of the windows within his view were lit, displaying rectangular yellow interiors, noiseless genre scenes of pasta pots, embracing or retreating couples, cats, squabbles, and, three houses down, a solitary smoker sitting in the dark by an open window, cigarette end glowing scarlet.

He wrapped up the stirring conversation with Fiona, then took a drag on his own cigarette and tipped his head back to exhale, looking up at a jeweled airplane in the sky, following its trajectory hungrily with his eyes even though he had only two days ago returned from Belarus and would be off again in two days if not sooner to Haiti.

Adrenalin junkies was what they called themselves, he and his fellow foreign correspondents. It was undeniably addictive, the lure of being away, of being witness to the unfolding of important events, and also of being in some heady way exempt. At the end of the day, with any luck at all they went back to their foreign correspondents' hotel and had a drink together.

He was exempt at home, too. He could not be expected to latch straight back into the mundane daily round after what he had seen. So when Barbara in a crass moment asked him to do something like take out the rubbish, as she had tonight, it jarred.

"Sorry, I was miles away," he'd said. "Can't get that child out of my mind, the one I was telling you about who lost both her legs in the bombing. What did you say?"

"Nothing," Barbara had mumbled, tying up the black plastic sack.

Anyway, she'd left him alone to take care of Daisy for fifty minutes this afternoon while she went off to do some shopping or whatever. "Bond with your daughter!" she'd ordered, heavily waggish, before disappearing off to do whatever it was she wanted to do. She was crap at jokes.

There was no guilt. Feelings are, after all, involuntary. The holiness of the heart's affections, and so on. As Fiona said, it was ridiculous to talk about someone else breaking up a marriage; a marriage would have to be in trouble already for the husband to want to sleep with someone else. Or the wife, she'd added, scrupulously fair.

Not that any boats had yet been burned. Or launched, for that matter; Fiona was a tad too cut and dried to get romantic about. Thing was, he wanted his cake and eat it. Barbara could be a wet blanket all right, nothing to talk about except the child and the dripping tap. On the other hand, he wouldn't actually like to live with one of the Fionas. As that guy from Reuters had said one night when they were getting out of it on the local champagne, what you wanted when you were fresh back from a war zone was a vase of flowers and your dinner on the table, not some ambitious female cutting you up at the lights— "Oh yeah, I'm off to Tashkent tomorrow," that sort of thing.

Even so, it was only his second night back and already they were reduced to penne with pesto and frozen peas. I could have stayed in Belarus for that, he'd joked. She blamed it on the traffic and Daisy teething; and then she sat gnawing her cuticles while he drank his coffee. When he asked her not to, she proceeded to play with her hair instead, using a strand to floss her teeth when she thought he wasn't looking. She couldn't keep her hands still, it was probably her most infuriating habit, they were always up near her face, her mouth, her hair; if he snapped at her to keep them below shoulder level she would sit with them in her lap and twist her wedding ring round and round.

That really got to him. She'd been doing it tonight.

He decided on one last cigarette before going in. It was the sovereign cure. Not only did it make his irritation melt away, but it dropped his shoulders and sharpened his mind so that he started to concentrate on the Belarus piece, even scribbled a few words onto the back of his Marlboro packet.

That done, he inhaled luxuriously and toyed with certain useful clichés. "I need some space" was so obviously code for something else, like "I need some time alone," that its use these days was the lazy man's insult. "Life is not a dress rehearsal" was more interesting because, while widely used as a get-out clause, what it really meant was "I'm about to do something incredibly rash and ill-advised." No, the loftiest current euphemism had to be "Time to move on." That would do if it came to it. Dignified, nonspecific, fabulously exculpatory. Time to move on. There was no answer to that.

He shivered. It had been a moody day, typical April in England, half hours of hot sun then quick banks of cool storm clouds draining the light. It was cold now. Grinding his cigarette stub into the grass, he groaned inwardly and went indoors.

"The only appointment they have is at eight twenty," said Barbara, appearing beside him with a cup of tea.

"What time is it?" he murmured, keeping his eyes shut against her.

"Seven thirty-five. I've been up since five with Daisy, it's her teeth again. But I really think you should go, Tom, he said you should go back within two weeks if it didn't clear up but you've been away so much it's more like two months . . ."

"Yeah yeah yeah," said Tom, hauling himself up against the pillows.

The trouble with Barbara was that she made such a production out of being a misery. She huffed, she sighed, her face drooped with reproach whenever she saw him. Or, mute appeal was how she would probably put it. It was a habit she couldn't kick and, as he told her, every bit as bad as his smoking, which she went on about incessantly.

Right on cue he broke into a brief harsh fit of coughing.

"You see? I worry about you, flying all the time and the superbugs in the air-conditioning."

"But eight twenty. Christ."

"I'm sorry, darling, it's the only one they had, I had to make it a same-day appointment, they keep a few open every morning and you have to wait in the phone queue at seven thirty to get one," she intoned, drawing the curtains.

"Okay, okay," he said.

She had a bloody nice life, part-time and all the rest of it, yet she was ravenous for pity, addicted to it. He even had to commiserate with her, for fuck's sake, he actually had to join in with her moaning on about what a hard row she had to hoe before she'd let him get his leg over.

"And I couldn't make you an ordinary appointment because they're booking three weeks ahead and we never know what you'll be doing in three weeks' time. Couldn't you have a word at work about that? Little Daisy never knows when she'll be seeing you . . ."

"Shut *up*," said Tom softly, eyes closed, sucking in his first draft of tea.

"It's only you I'm thinking of."

She was hurt now; but then, when wasn't she?

"Reach me my fags," he demanded, silently daring her to deliver them with a health lecture. He kept his eyes shut. There was a long pause.

"Fuck's sake, I'll go to the quack at eight twenty. Now give me my cigarettes," he said, opening one eye to menace her with.

With a gusty sigh she brought them to him.

"You promise?" she said.

"Yes," he said, lighting up.

There came a yell from Daisy in her cot.

"Smoking can cause a slow and painful death," she quoted, scurrying from the bedroom.

"Careful, darling, don't go giving me ideas," he muttered.

I arrive on time, they're late, he thought, tapping his foot, looking round with distaste at the waiting room full of sore-eyed sneezers and losers. He was down to see a Dr. Cooling and didn't know whether this would be a man or a woman. It had been a man when he came six weeks ago. A viral infection of the respiratory tract, he'd announced. Brilliant.

"It still hasn't cleared up," he said to Dr. Cooling, who turned out to be an uncharming young female with little glasses like arrow slits.

"Smoker?"

"Yes, but I think it's a bug I've picked up abroad."

"How long?"

"How long what?"

"How long have you been a smoker?"

"What's that got to do with it? Since I was fifteen. Fourteen."

She tapped something into the computer, then gave him a cursory examination with a stethoscope.

"Any blood in the sputum?"

"There has been a bit, probably just broken capillaries because it's a really hacking cough, this one."

"Night sweats?"

"Look, I've been in a war zone for the last week, I simply wouldn't notice something like that," he said. You tended to be more concerned about landmines and snipers than your nicotine intake, was what he wanted to convey. She was remarkably unresponsive. He had, actually, been waking drenched in sweat in the small hours for a while now.

"Weight loss?"

"Some," he said grudgingly. "But that goes with the job. Pot noodles and cold baked beans can take the edge off your appetite."

She glanced at her watch.

"I'd like you to go along for an X-ray," she said, scribbling something on a pad. "You don't need to book, just turn up at the hospital and wave this form. We'll let you know when we get the results if you need to see us again."

She wouldn't give him any drugs; told him to take acetaminophen if his chest hurt. Great. Waste of time, he told Barbara when he got home.

A week later, when he got back from Haiti, there was a letter asking him to come in and discuss the X-ray results. Barbara once again arranged a same-day appointment for him.

"So what does a shadow on the lung actually mean?" he asked Dr. Minton, a middle-aged man this time, breezy and positive. "It sounds like something out of a Victorian novel."

"It may mean nothing very much," twinkled Dr. Minton, indicating the darker claw-shaped area spread over the upper lobes of the lung X-ray. "But just to be on the safe side I'd like you to go for a few more tests."

"I'm off to Malawi on Wednesday," said Tom. "Can't it wait?"

"I really do think it would be a good idea to get the tests done as soon as possible," Dr. Minton said, looking hard at the backs of his hands. "By all means let's see if we can't fast-track it. Does your work provide health insurance?"

And so, within forty-eight hours, Tom was sitting opposite Mr. Orlando Horton, one of London's leading respiratory physicians. Between them was Mr. Horton's immense desk. Mr. Horton was himself immense, a great gloomy tree of a man. When Tom had first entered the room, the tree had advanced toward him with out-stretched hand, and Tom, who was over six feet tall, had found himself looking up at him like a child. He must be six six, thought Tom now, stupidly; six seven.

"So what do you think this shadow thing is?" he had asked him, cheerfully enough.

"I think it is lung cancer," Mr. Horton had said in a grave voice, lacing his long white surgeon's fingers together on his blotter.

"Cancer?" Tom had yelped.

"Of course I cannot give a cast-iron diagnosis until the results of your bronchoscopy and sputum tests are on my desk. But that is what it looks like to me."

"Cancer?" Tom had repeated, in more of a bleat this time.

"I'm sorry if this has come as a shock to you," said Mr. Horton. "But I believe in telling the truth."

"Oh so do I," Tom had agreed, nodding his head vigor-ously. "The truth is very, yes, absolutely."

Mr. Horton had gone on talking but Tom somehow hadn't heard what he was saying. The man was huge. There was something of Belgium about him, the lack of life in the streets, the uncurtained windows. He saw him lurking in some airless Victorian interior crammed with greedy aspidistra plants, more outside in the garden, gluttonous evergreens, fat rank graveyard swathes of ivy and laurel and yew. An arboretum, murmured Tom, a pinetum.

"Sorry?"

"No, no," said Tom. "Carry on."

He was interested to see how Mr. Horton was pushing himself further and further back from his desk during this consultation. He was almost backing out of the window by the end. You could imagine him as a child waiting for punishment, enormous in shorts, lugubrious, at Eton or one of those places where they made you line up outside the door then show your bottom. But he was up again with his hand stuck out to be shaken, and it seemed it was time to be off.

"Very often people do not take in everything I have told them," the talking tree said mournfully. "Should you find this to be your own case, my secretary will give you written details of where to go and so on for the further tests I have advised."

"Thank you," said Tom, pumping his hand witlessly and grinning like a zany.

He found himself gasping for a cigarette, trembling all over with desire and need, but smoking was banned on the Underground. There was this unattractive female waiting beside him on the bench, and she was eating a bean salad with brown rice and smelly vinaigrette. She was oblivious to the fact that the smell of her food was turning people away from her, that she was hogging the bench. She ate carefully and greedily, chasing the last recalcitrant beans round the plastic box with her metal fork. (More than twenty-five years of heavy smoking, Mr. Treetrunk had said, shaking his head.) She must have cooked it and packed it the night before. No make-up, a bogbrush hairdo, but she knew what was good for her and she was looking after her health. Tom hated her with all his heart. He had to move away in case he took her fork off her and stabbed her with it.

He walked back home from the station, through the park, looking around him with peeled eyes. All about him were the cherry cheeks and Lycra of people out doing themselves good. He stopped to examine the criss-crossed cablelike flexibility of some late catkins. Plants! They were incredible. Look at the shape of that leaf! The wasteful little knots and garlands of buds gave him pause, some like fat beads and others full but pointed, little pleated leaves still fresh, not quite unpacked. All winter these trees had stood bare-boned, and now this. It wasn't fair.

Barbara was wonderful. When he got back to the house and told her, she went white, then held him hard in her arms. It was gratifying, frankly.

He lay winded on the sofa while she sat on the floor

beside him and clasped his hands, kissing them, her face concealed by the pale curtain of her hair.

"I just didn't take any of it in after he'd told me it was lung cancer," he said. "I don't honestly remember anything. I think the secretary gave me some bits of paper about tests. Christ, I'd better look up my pension details. Work. What do I do about work? I'm supposed to be in Malawi in two days. How long have I got? I mean, here on the planet, as opposed to London or wherever."

"We should find out what we can," said Barbara. "Some facts. Statistics. Then maybe we can work out what it is we have to face."

He loved her sanity, her gravity, her sweet round face and long fair hair like an early Flemish madonna. There was something a little disquieting about the way she was rising to the occasion, as though it was what she'd been waiting for all these years, but he brushed that thought aside and concentrated on the way she'd said *we* and not *you*.

Gingerly they surfed the Net together. Carcinogens in cigarette smoke cause nearly nine in ten deaths from lung cancer. Abnormal cells dividing uncontrollably. Traveling in the blood and lymph. Secondary tumors. Metastasis. Chemotherapy. Palliative care. The five-year survival rate, so hopeful in testicular cancer at nine in ten, was here more like one in twenty.

"Let's turn off the computer," said Barbara.

"Too much information," quipped Tom. Everything felt speeded up, as though he were in a cartoon.

"Let's wait until your next appointment with the consultant," said Barbara. "It's not long, we can get our questions ready for him then."

The cartoon quality stayed with him while she went to collect Daisy from the nursery. He was fascinated by this stroke of ill fortune, how to take it, how to absorb it, in what posture to meet it. He was used to catastrophes, but only to the catastrophes of others. Now he had one of his own. What was it you said in this situation, wasn't there some phrase? I've had a good innings, that was it, to show you were a good sport. No, he couldn't say that.

My number's up. That was better. He saw himself in a paddleboat on a pond, as a megaphoned voice ordered, "Come in number seven, your time is up." Then he saw himself frantically paddling the boat away to the far shore, trying to escape the black-cowled park keeper.

They were back. Daisy ran to him and he stooped to pick her up and swing her in the air. The child, the poor child, he thought; they're so defenseless, children. She laughed with surprise as he whirled her round the room, and he wondered why he hadn't noticed before that emergent blue-white frill of tooth. She would soon be fatherless.

"How will she remember me?" he asked Barbara, and

answered before she could—"With a cigarette hanging out of my mouth." He swore then and there that he would never smoke again. He shuddered at his selfish self of yesterday, this morning; found it inconceivable that he should have puffed away so blithely, poisoning the air where his own baby daughter was growing.

"How do I tell people?" he asked.

"Let's not tell anyone yet," said Barbara.

How wise she was, and how patient and kind! It was a bloody good job one of them was patient and kind—where would their poor child be otherwise? He saw now that these were the qualities he needed in a woman, the timeless womanly qualities of fidelity and selflessness and compassion. Plus, he couldn't help but add, full-time nursing skills. How could he have berated her for being boring? Stimulation he could do without, he got enough of that at work, surely. There were always books for fuck's sake. It was the balance of the yin and the yang, they'd had their own dynamic all along; he saw that now.

There was one other person he felt he had to tell.

"It's not something for over the phone," he muttered into his cell phone from inside the garden shed. He had offered to unearth Daisy's tricycle and have another go at teaching her how to use it. Well, a first go, if he was honest.

"That sounds intriguing," came Fiona's laid-back drawl.

She was less amused when he told her his news over a glass of wine at her flat. She stopped looking sleek and smiling and pleased with herself. Her face went blank as though a cloud had gone over the sun.

"The thing about lung cancer is that the, ah, prognosis is not good. The outlook."

"I know what prognosis means," she said, lowering her beautiful eyelids.

"And yet the extraordinary thing is, I keep forgetting for a moment and imagining everything's all right again. You know, like when there's five minutes of blue sky after a month of rain and immediately you assume it's going to stay like that for good."

"Mmm," said Fiona, sipping her wine.

"There's this deep brainless underlying optimism," said Tom with a shaky laugh.

"You're in denial," said Fiona in a flat voice. "There are four stages, you know. Denial, anger, depression, acceptance. You're still in the first."

"Not really. God, I wake in the night and it's real enough then. Why me and all that. Why me."

"You should stop being such a victim and take control of your treatment," Fiona opined, and this time there was no mistaking the tone of her voice.

"Victim?" spluttered Tom.

Her revulsion was palpable. When he reached across and touched her neck, she got up and crossed the room to get away from him.

"It's not catching, you know," he said.

"Why don't you try that juice cure," she said, lighting a cigarette. "Flush all the toxins out."

"Forgive me," he murmured into Barbara's hair that night.

"What for?"

"I haven't been very . . . I've taken you for granted."

She had had a lot to put up with over the years, he saw that now. He felt remorse for the times when he had been unkind and, yes actually, even cruel. Now that he was about to be plucked away from it, his life with her seemed foolishly underappreciated. The boats were burned at last, if not in the way he had envisaged.

Gone were thoughts of sexual boredom. Gratefully he dived into Barbara. Vanished was his chilliness toward the under-threes. Ardently he courted Daisy, dazzling her with his funny faces and noises and tricks. Held in the unaccustomed beam of his goodwill, their smiles were pleased but cautious.

Four in the morning became the new time of waking. It was obviously an unconscious urge to be sentient for as much of his remaining non-ash time as possible. He wavered on the threshold of how to face the future. Would he brave it out with stoicism? Or not? The ideal held up for a dying man was of a good-humored lack of self-mourning. Yet, was it really such a virtue not to mind? Or to lie and claim you didn't mind? It would be a gallant pulling of the wool over the eyes to let the living off the hook by not showing pain or fear; but on the other hand, they weren't the ones on the way out.

I'm crocked, he thought, hands behind his head and staring up at the ceiling; I'm finished. From some bleak dawn corner of his brain came the new voice.

—Go to sleep quietly; you knew all along it ended like this. For everybody. Who cares? In the end, so what. Who do you think you are? Why should you matter?

He listened to Barbara's breathing and felt her warm thigh against his.

—Who cares? Friends? Family? Your other half?

—Yes no yes.

—Harm and grief. You don't want to rip them out of their own lives.

—I do.

—Is life so fabulous after all?

—Yes.

—All the same, you'll be dead soon, whether you like it or not. You know that, don't you?

He lay there and waited, and gradually gray light crept above the curtains across the ceiling.

If, he vowed in his mind, *if* I am spared, never again will I complain about anything. I will accept life as it comes and I will not waste any more of it in pandering to the greedy restless self. I see it all now, how it is and how life should be lived.

Barbara came with him to the next appointment. She paused at the majestic front door to breathe on the brass plaque where clusters of letters swarmed after Mr. Orlando Horton's name.

"Impressive, eh?" said Tom. "They're called mister only when they're really top of the pile. He's obviously one of the best men for what I've got, at least there is that."

He broke off into a fit of coughing, and spat the frightening blood-flecked results into a tissue. Barbara turned her head away and reached for more tissues. She handed him one and dabbed at her tears with another.

"Do I look as though I've been crying?" she asked.

"Not at all," he lied, moved by the scarlet and turquoise of her eyes, and drew her into him, tucking her bowed head beneath his chin.

Fifteen minutes later they were standing out on the steps again in a very different state.

"You haven't got cancer," said Barbara, clutching his hand, his loose fist, and moving it with little rocking movements along her cheek, under her jaw. She hung on to his hand and kissed it.

"I'm not going to die," marveled Tom. He had his arm round her shoulders, sagged onto her.

"You'll get better," sniffed Barbara, holding his hand to her wet face. She wouldn't let go.

"It'll take five sets of drugs," said Tom. "A cocktail of drugs as he put it. But there's no question. They'll work."

"Tuberculosis!" marveled Barbara. "I thought it had disappeared."

"I can't believe it," he said, propelling her down to the pavement. "Let's find somewhere for coffee."

"Did he actually say he'd made a mistake at any point?" asked Barbara, her face in ruins after the last half hour, ruins through which the sun now shone.

"No, he didn't, did he?" said Tom, halting again.

"It was when he said, 'In retrospect,' " said Barbara. "Then I knew there was a chance."

"In retrospect," said Tom. "You're right. It's one of those phrases. Same as, 'With the benefit of hindsight.' Bastard. Why didn't I say anything? I just felt so stunned. I'm going back in right now."

"Oh, Tom, please," said Barbara. "You're alive. I need a coffee."

"In retrospect," snarled Tom, leading her off to the nearest Starbucks.

That afternoon they had a celebration with Daisy; they collected her from the nursery and sat out on the pocket handkerchief of lawn in the back garden with a cake and candles. "Happy birthday," sang Daisy, and Barbara couldn't stop smiling. I've been allowed back on, thought Tom. When Daisy blew out the candles, he lit them again. I didn't want to have to get off the train yet, he thought, and in the end I didn't have to. Barbara cut the cake into slices, and he ate more than his fair share, though neither she nor Daisy seemed to mind.

Some weeks later, one fine warm evening late in May, Tom was standing out in the garden. It was almost dark, and Barbara was at the back door. She'd been nagging him about taking more time off, but nothing was going to stop him from leaving tomorrow, early. He was off to Islamabad and had just been informed that the lovely Sophie would be coming along as research assistant.

"Tom," called Barbara softly from the back door.

"In a minute," he replied.

She had been doing that thing she did. After they'd eaten their pasta, in the space where normally he'd be enjoying a cigarette with his coffee, she'd been fiddling with her wedding ring, twisting it round and round. It drove him mad. Why did she carry on doing it when she knew how much it irritated him? Then, when she thought he wasn't looking, he saw her floss the gap between her front teeth with a strand of her long hair.

From his jeans pocket now he extracted the contraband pack of Marlboro. There was the brief flare of a match in the dark, then the end of his cigarette glowed scarlet. He pulled out his cell phone and tapped in a number. As he waited for the connection he took a draft of nicotine, bathing himself like a Roman emperor in its fabulous drench.

"Is that Sophie?" he murmured. "Ah, just the goddess I wanted to talk to. Now, tell me . . ."

He was standing in the lush dusk of early summer, his shoes white with petals in grass still wet from the afternoon rain. The yellow-lit windows of the terraced houses opposite were silent pictures of talk and appetite and solitude. All round the back gardens the candles of horse chestnut trees glowed creamy in the gloom and a soft marzipan scent blew from their clusters over and around him. He didn't really notice any of that; he was too busy talking, soft and urgent, into his cell phone.

The Phlebotomist's
Love Life

Sun slid early over the curtains and woke her still smiling from their victorious photo finish of the night before. They had been together for a year and together was the word. She saw now that without this private truthful allying in powerful pairs all over the globe, without this nothing would work and the world would come to an end. Then came the tide of unease like a body blush, the flush of dismay. What had they done in the night? She flicked on the radio and he moaned in his sleep beside her.

"Sorry," she whispered, remembering he was on a late, and slipped off to the kitchen with her work clothes. She put some toast on and filled the kettle. "Has he killed as many people as Stalin?" came the voice from the radio, keen as mustard. "Proportionately, that is?"

How eager they had all been to step out of the blood-boltered twentieth century, she thought as she pulled on her tights; how sick to the back teeth of the fangs of history and misery they all were. Now look. Some belle epoque. Not even one prelapsarian decade this time; not even one paltry year of peace.

Stopping at the cornershop to buy a paper, she scanned the photos beneath the headlines on display, palm trees and oily black cumulus clouds and silent howling faces.

"Lovely morning," said Ahmed as she paid him.

"Beautiful," she agreed. "Terrible," she added, indicating the front page of her paper.

"Terrible, terrible," muttered Ahmed. "The poor people. What have they done? They have done nothing."

She stifled the impulse to apologize. He, too, presumably, had helped to vote in this government.

On the bus it was standing room only. It had always caused her trouble with men—war. She dreaded its approach, from the moment when they first mentioned its possibility on the news to the pretend discussion about rights and wrongs in the run-up. She remembered her first proper boyfriend, Ewan, and his rage at her objections to the Gulf War. True, her talk had sounded childish even to her, even then when she was only twenty—wishing that women could go off and live on another continent, man-free, war-free. Or, at least, go to that neutral continent taking the children with them for the duration of any war the men had created. Without testosterone and the desire for phallic toys, she'd argued, the world would be a better place.

Bollocks, he'd said.

Who had she been with during the Kosovo conflict? With Dan, of course. War is the worst, she'd told him; living in a state of murder and the reversal of all things good.

What about the Second World War? he demanded. Eh? Wasn't that a just war? You'd have been wringing your hands along with Neville Chamberlain, wouldn't you, all out for appeasement.

At times like this, she cried, women get put in their place. They go horribly quiet. It comes down to rape and babies. Ah, ah, you don't like me going on at you like this. You'd prefer me in a chador! A burka!

You're like a fox terrier, aren't you? he'd said when she'd continued to disagree with him; you get hold of an idea and then nothing'll stop the yapping.

Up on the fifth floor in Hematology, they were slopping around with their early-morning caffe lattes and setting up for the day ahead. Ambulance sirens hooted like owls, the noise drifting up from the roads round the hospital. She took her own coffee to a grime-streaked window and looked down over the waking city, its tower blocks and churches and grids of terraced houses spread out to the sun, some hundreds of thousands of lives within her purlieu, and as she looked her eye's imagination pumped clouds of poison in an unnerving pall across the landscape.

Soon there were twenty or so patients clutching numbered paper tickets in the waiting room where she was. Her job was to take blood, but not till nine o'clock and it was still only five to. A mournful-faced elderly man appeared at the door, clutching a big pink plastic-covered number eight.

"Is this where I should be?" he asked.

"No, you're a Warfarin if you've been given that plastic number," she told him. "You want the anticoagulant clinic down on the third floor."

"Are you sure?" he said. "This is the blood department, isn't it? Some other young woman assured me it was up here."

"Well, yes, this is one part of it but you need the other part, and that's on the third floor."

"Just my luck. The lift's broken."

"There's one that works on the other side of the building," she told him. "If you walk along that corridor, follow it along to the swing doors, then keep left."

I'll never believe the government again when it says there's no money for public services, she thought; not after this, not after it's written a blank check to the army without a murmur.

In her side room of sharps and Vacutainers she passed her working days in a sequence of three-minute cycles. Hello! she said with a reassuring smile. Yes, one arm out of a sleeve please; some random chat if they wanted that while she hunted for the vein, then they looked away, often talking rapidly while she slowly drew off a dark crimson tubeful. Occasionally someone would express surprise at the blood being purple-crimson, and she would take another half minute to explain that this was venous blood as opposed to the oxygenated arterial scarlet sort that flows from cuts and wounds.

These days, rather than quiz them about holiday plans before she inserted the needle, she simply said in a neutral voice: "So what do you think of the war, then." She found the daily montage of opinion this tactic produced addictively compelling.

It's all wrong that they're e-mailing home, said one; soldiers should cut off from the soft domestic side of things, they shouldn't be thinking about whether their boy was Man of the Match; you know he sends his football team to be tortured if they lose? I'm fifty, said another, and this is the first time in my life I've felt ashamed of my country; I wake up and I feel ashamed. War is inevitable, shrugged the third in line, it's part of human nature; they haven't had one for a while. *Why* is war inevitable? fumed the next one on; who *says?* People no longer fight duels to settle arguments, so why continue to do so at a national level? There are other ways to get what you want.

"Here we all are," declared a stout well-dressed old man, "we've been managing to live alongside Muslims for the last thousand years—and now this! Don't they know anything? Haven't they read *any* history? Ouch." He rolled his eyes up to the sky with dismal sarcasm. "Maybe *Jesus* will save us."

"Everybody's got used to it now, because it's not affecting our lives here," claimed a large woman with a toddler in tow. "We're all still doing what we normally do. It's awful really, the way the children sit in front of the television and say, 'Oh, not the war again,' and zap it with the remote. Ben, put that down. *Now.*"

He's a vile dictator and he cannot be allowed to go on torturing and murdering his own people and manufacturing chemical weapons, she was told; he's in breach of UN resolutions; he's a menace to everyone and it's high time he was taken out.

Surely there are other ways of saving a country than by making it uninhabitable, she heard; what they've spent on bombs in the last fortnight would have covered the cost of providing clean water for the entire world.

Her last of the morning was American, heavily pregnant and incandescent with indignation. "It's like a bad dream," she cried, not waiting to be prompted, "but the trouble is when I wake up each morning I realize it's not a dream. You know he's from Texas? Did you know it's legal there to carry a gun but against the law to own a vibrator? Make war not love, hey! I'm glad I'm not in the war zone right now, I'd be in the line of pregnant women at the hospital begging for a Cesarian. Cluster bombs, shrapnel, did you see that bus they bombed last night, killed eight children, the baby in a shroud . . ."

"Shhh, shhh," she said to her once she'd sealed up her blood and put it safely to one side. She handed her a tissue. "You mustn't think about it for the next few days, you must avoid the papers and the news generally or your blood pressure will go sky high and they'll haul you in for observation and you don't want *that*."

"Right," agreed the woman, blowing her nose. "But it's hard not to think about it all the time, you know?"

Down in the staff canteen, she took her tray of lasagne over to a table of her friends.

"Very anti this morning," she said as she sat down. "Five for, sixteen against, three undecided."

"You could be on to a nice little earner there," said Agnes. "You should get on to Gallup Poll or whoever it is that comes up with these statistics."

"Preemptive strike," said Femi as she reached across and grabbed the last roll.

"Widespread confusion and dismay," she added. "Nobody's very happy about it. It's as though the national autoimmune system was starting to pack up. I still haven't met anyone who knows what it's *for.*"

"Can we not talk about the war for a change?" asked Femi plaintively. "Look, I've got pictures of my new niece to show you."

"She's gorgeous," said Agnes, studying the proffered photographs. "She's scrumptious. She's got a face like a flower." Agnes was gentle and indecisive generally, a dove if ever there was one, but had flown out hawkishly over the war. Her brother-in-law had been in his prisons, and though she would not say what had happened to him there Agnes thought even war was better than letting such things exist.

But if we remove one tyrant, then why not another, she'd said to Agnes; most of the staff at this hospital could give ample reason for us to go to war with their country of origin—every single one of them, if you were to ask the cleaners.

True, said Agnes; and maybe that's the way ahead.

"She's her third," said Femi. "My sister says that's it, three girls are as much as she can cope with. But I tell her not to be so sure, her husband's always on about wanting a boy to play football with."

Three girls, she thought. Three girls in pinafores and four boys with side-partings her great-grandmother had raised—the hundred-year-old photograph was in a shoe-box at home somewhere. One son had been killed in each year of the First World War. Apparently their mother had not done much after 1918; there was nothing physically wrong with her but after the last boy was killed she hadn't really gotten out of bed, though she'd lived another thirty years, tended by her daughters.

"Room for a little one?" said two-hundred-pound Patricia, fellow phlebotomist, breezing up with a plate of fish and chips. "I've been taking blood all morning in a drafty old church hall and I'm starving."

"Aren't they letting us have the school gym anymore?" she asked.

"No, they decided the little bleeders were missing too much PE so that was that," said Patricia, shaking on the vinegar. "Joke, ladies, joke. We're allowed to say bloody and bleeder, perks of the job."

"Is it because stocks are low?" asked Agnes. "Is it because of the war?"

"They're always a bit low," said Patricia, tucking in. "People are squeamish, Tony Hancock's got a lot to answer for. As well as the other one. So yes, supplies can always do with being beefed up, and of course blood doesn't store terribly well, it's got a shelf life of only a week or two."

"I would like to give blood," said Femi.

"Good for you," said Patricia. "Though honestly,

they've turned it into such a palaver that if you're not careful it'll take you half a day rather than half an hour; you have to fill in questionnaires about drugs and travel and whether you've had a new sexual partner in the last three months, and you can't be on any sort of medication."

"Hmm," said Femi. "I wouldn't have to take the time as holiday, would I?"

"I'll do you upstairs after lunch, love, if they can spare you over in Casualty," said Patricia. "You'll have to wait till I've had my pudding, though."

"So what do *you* think of the war, then, Patricia?" she asked, despite herself.

"She can't leave it alone, that one," tutted Femi.

"It feels wrong because we started it and it wasn't in self-defense," said Patricia. "And it feels perverse because we're not going to get anything out of it; least of all safety or honor. Not bleeding likely. *That's* what I think."

"Nobody will join the army after this," she said, staring at images of dust and tanks and gunfire.

"Oh, but they will," he said. "Of course they will. They'll sign up in their thousands. This is what you want if you're attracted to the army. What's the point if you don't get to fight? Especially if you're on the side with the best guns and you know you've got a hundred times the firepower of the enemy."

"But how can they want this?" she asked.

"What?" he said, half listening.

"How can they want *this*."

"Men like fighting," he said simply, staring at the screen. "They always have. Action. Competition, aggression, call it what you like."

"What?" she said.

"The challenge. Adrenalin. Fitness, strength. Pitting yourself against the enemy. Targets. Explosions."

He picked up the remote control and pointed it at the television.

Mothers repeating their grief, she thought. If she had a son, where would she hide him? She imagined a future call-up, the open-faced conscripts; a quick horrid fantasy of fear and protections; taking milk to the cellar.

"You'd want a boy," she said. "Wouldn't you? You would."

"What?" he said, absently, staring at the little brightly colored manikins that had appeared on the screen. "Oh! Nice one!"

He had been flipping between channels for a while now, the flares and flashes and explosions changing place with roaring and balls and goals. Men are for Mars, she thought; is *that* it?

"Can't you stay with one channel?" she asked.

"I just wanted to see how Arsenal were doing."

"Come on the Gunners!" she sneered.

"What?" he said, startled.

"I don't know what you think about the war," she said. "You never talk to me."

"Yes, I do!" he said, rising to the attack.

"We only ever watch television and go to bed."

"No, we don't!"

"Yes, we do," she said. Oh yes, we do. Were they clowns arguing in a pantomime?

"Look, I'm tired. I've had a long day. But if you want to 'talk'—*fine*," he said. He pressed the MUTE button on the remote control; not the OFF button, she noticed; the football was in its eighty-third minute. "What about?"

"The war," she said.

He made a noise somewhere between fury and disgust.

"I just can't believe you get so angry when I try to talk to you about the war," she said.

"I'm not angry," he said. "You just go on and on."

"Don't hate me," she said. "I put up with sitting in front of hours of football because I love sitting with your arm round me and my head on your shoulder."

"I don't hate you," he said. "I love you."

"I know. But I need to know what you think about the war because we're part of each other."

"Right. Yes. This is what I think. If it's over fast, with few civilian casualties, there will be a feeling of it's all been worth it. It was justified. Whereas if it goes on for months and eats up the national budget and there are more casualties on both sides than expected, then it will *not* be seen as good."

"But what do *you* feel?"

"I've just told you!"

"What, so how it turns out will justify it or not?"

"Yes."

"But surely there are first principles? The end doesn't justify the means?"

"I've said what I think," he shrugged, his eyes back on the screen. He pressed a button and the crowd started roaring again.

Even she could see that she wasn't going to get any more out of him in the eighty-sixth minute of the game; and it wouldn't be just four minutes to wait, it always went into extra time. She decided to get ready for bed. In the shower she soaped and scrubbed and loudly sang until the tiles echoed—"And another one gone and another one gone, another one bites the dust . . ."

In bed, he turned to her and held her. Don't mention the war must be her motto now, on the home front at least. He buried his face in her neck. She stiffened and willed herself not to shrug him off. If she stayed with him, she'd have to button her lip. He put his hands in her hair and his mouth on hers, and moved to lie on top of her. At this point usually her arms would clasp him and her legs twine round his as she returned his kisses; but now she found herself heaving his weight off with unexpected violence.

"What's the matter?" he asked, baffled.

"I don't know," she said, sitting up.

"Nothing's the matter," he murmured. "Come here," and pulled her back down to him.

"Don't," she said loudly, surprising them both.

"What?" he said.

"My body can't pretend," she found herself saying. "You always said you liked that about me. My body can't tell lies."

"What?" he said again, trying to draw her to him.

"Unless you're happy with forcing legs open and spit in your face," she hissed. "Yes, you *would* like that, I bet."

"No," he said, aghast.

"Then you can just fuck off," she said.

"What?" he said.

But she had already left the bedroom, slamming the door behind her. She stormed off to the sofa and to late-night television. There, she lay down and watched the war and wept.

The Green Room

A fat woman with a frozen shoulder sat sighing by the steady flames of a fake-coal fire. At her feet crowded a congregation of coffee-dregged mugs, dead wine bottles, and ashtrays crammed with crushed stubs. Across the room a television chattered gravely, on screen a long face in *contre-jour* against a scene of bloody devastation; over in the corner crouched a computer caught short mid-document.

"I must get on," said this woman, Pamela, not moving. Piles of paper fanned out across the floor, lists and reports and unwritten Christmas cards, bills and charity fliers and unopened correspondence including a parcel about the size of a shoebox wrapped in brown paper. This last item now catching her eye, she leaned over and picked it up.

"Munich," she said, reading the postmark. "That'll be cousin Gerda again with another bit of tat from the Christmas market. Why on earth does she bother?"

Sure enough, it was a decoration for her tree, the tree that was still on her to-do list, unbought as yet, and this time it was some sort of angel or fairy with a schmaltzy smile on its face. As she turned it over in her hands she noticed something printed on the hem of its stiff gold robe. The letters blurred beneath her bleary eyes and she had to hunt for her glasses before she was able to read what was printed there: www.festivelifecoach.com.

"Some sort of gimmick," she scoffed, but in the end could not resist going over to her computer to log on, this gimmick having stirred her listlessness into action where lists alone had failed. As soon as she had entered the address there flashed up the following words:

Change your life!
Suspend your disbelief!
Press ctrl + esc at the same time while holding down the shift key. Close your eyes and when you hear the sound of bells tap in "3D" and wait. Keep your eyes closed until you hear the instruction to open them or your computer will crash irretrievably and forever.

Pamela frowned, gave a scornful laugh, and paused a long moment; then she breathed in, pressed the specified keys, and closed her eyes.

As she waited, she thought of the time she was wasting and ground her teeth. This was the story of her life, a mountain of stuff waiting to be done and her somehow not doing it and not even enjoying not doing it, in fact finding it even more exhausting and depressing not doing it than doing it. She had to send that report off by this evening; what did she think she was playing at now, standing in the middle of the room with her eyes shut like a fool?

At this point her unhappy reverie was broken by a peal of bells, and the stale air of her sitting room thinned to frosty silver in her nostrils. She breathed slowly, followed the instructions as they were given, and at last opened her eyes.

In front of her stood a small spry figure in a scarlet tracksuit and emerald sneakers. Radiating aerobic bonhomie, it held a branch of fresh green holly in its hand. "I must have dozed off in front of the fire after all," she said, pinching herself dispassionately.

"No, you didn't," smiled the creature. "You called me up on the Internet, and now I am here to help you slip your mind-forged manacles. My name is—can you guess?" and here it waved the green branch playfully. "Holly!"

"What?" she said.

"Let's not waste time," beamed Holly, glancing at her watch. "I am your dedicated life coach but I'm here for a limited period only. And the first thing I need to do is to establish your general mind-set with the help of this checklist. So, if you'll just answer a few simple questions, we'll get started."

"Sorry?" she said.

"Say whatever comes into your mind, blurt it out without thinking," Holly instructed, ignoring her bafflement. "First question, what do you do when you hear carol singers?"

"Hide," said Pamela, falling in with the apparition's obvious command of the situation.

"And how do you feel when you see festive greenery?"

"Well, ivy is death and graveyards," she continued in the same vein, "and holly is worth it only when it's got berries and that means a hard winter so I'm unlikely to celebrate that."

"Is this glass half full or half empty?" asked the life coach, holding up a flute of red wine.

"Half empty, of course," said Pamela. "Can I have it please?"

"Lastly," said the life coach, handing her the glass, "what does the month of December mean to you?"

"Bleak weather. Leafless trees. The death of the year," said Pamela between sips. "Nervousness. Waiting to see where the shadow of the leather-winged reaper will fall. Then the chore of Christmas and downhill all the way to filthy February. So corny, so regular."

"Thank you," said the life coach, snapping her notebook shut. "Now, would you agree with me that you have low self-esteem?"

"If you mean, do I think I'm rubbish," she barked mirthlessly, "that's a yes."

"People with low self-esteem exert a detrimental effect on the world around them," said Holly. "Particularly at Christmas. Put simply, you're a downer, a drainer, a drag. Not that many party invitations, I imagine?"

"One or two," she lied, tears of hurt springing to her eyes. "Now you're going to list the virtues of positive thinking, I bet. Well, let me tell you, positive thinking is just papering over the cracks."

"Hmm," twinkled the life coach. "I want you now to remember your promise to suspend your disbelief and follow me. Underneath, we both know the real you is not a mumbling vessel of self-pity with unwashed hair and biscuit crumbs down her front."

"Well, thank you very much," said Pamela, brushing at her clothes.

"Time to marshal your resources!" she cried. "First, we'll choose you a slogan—' 'Tis the season to be jolly.' Jolly, right? I think you would agree that this is not what you are now. Jolly is what we are going to work toward."

"I hate that word," said Pamela. "*Jolly!* Hockey sticks and snobbish enthusiasm and Dickens."

"Interesting, your aversion," said Holly. "It comes from the Old Norse, *jol* or *yule,* meaning the twelve-day heathen midwinter festival. Maybe you'll like it better as a word if you remember some of its other meanings over the centuries—brave-hearted, showy, splendid, amorous, self-confident, and slightly intoxicated. Let *jolly* inspire you! Use it to help you remember key points in your strategy. *J*—Just do it. *O*—Organize yourself. *L*—Lighten up. *L*—Laugh at trouble. *Y*—"

"Oh, for goodness' sake," she snapped. "Spare me the acronyms!"

"Yoga, I was going to say," continued Holly imperturbably. "That shoulder of yours looks very stiff."

"It's frozen, actually," said Pamela haughtily. "Extremely painful at night and not getting any better. I haven't got round to going to the doctor's yet but I looked it up myself and it'll probably need a corticosteroid injection directly into the shoulder joint sometime soon. Agony. Even then it probably won't get better for a good two years."

"Hmm," said Holly. "That little speech encapsulates your current way of thinking perfectly. Stinking thinking, I call it. It's time for the three *P*s. Just breathe on this mirror here, would you, and see what you can make out through the mist."

Pamela did as she was told and found herself staring at a strange tableau. A large glum creature with down-turned mouth and tear-glazed eyes sat slumped, sighing and venting the occasional groan. At first it plucked disconsolately at the bloated leeches that clustered over its limbs, then, giving that up as a bad job, turned to the toaster on the table beside it. Every time a couple of slices popped up, this creature buttered them and threw them into the air. Scores of slices of toast lay over the carpet encircling its feet. They had all landed butter side down.

"Tell me, Holly, who is this nasty creature and what has it to do with me?" asked Pamela, struck by a worrying feeling that she had met it somewhere before.

"This is Pessimism," said Holly. "And here, look, here comes its cousin Procrastination."

A disheveled figure shuffled into view, hawking and spitting, heaving a swag bag marked HOURS, DAYS, WEEKS, ETC. Its nails were bitten to the quick, its watch was running slow, and a cigarette hung from its slack damp lower lip. When Pamela strained her ears she could hear it muttering, "I'll give up in the New Year. When I get round to buying some nicotine patches. That's when I'll do it." Somewhere about its person a cell phone erupted and, after patting various pockets bulging with unopened brown envelopes, it answered the call. "Later," it said. "Later. Yes, yes, I know I said today. But now it's tomorrow.

No. It must have gotten lost in the post." And it limped off in a fug of lame excuses.

"Look, look," said Holly as a third character, even more repellent, appeared on the scene. This one was a female invertebrate wearing a woolly robe embroidered with the words KICK ME and PUSHOVER and I DON'T MIND. She moved in a peculiar corkscrew way, trailing behind her a bandaged suppurating leg.

"This is Passivity," said Holly. "See how hideously twisted by adaptive behavior she has become."

"But what is the matter with her leg?" asked Pamela, struck by a physical affliction some degrees worse than her own.

"A couple of months ago she stubbed her toe and slowly it turned septic," said Holly. "She waited and waited for someone to tell her to go to the doctor but nobody did—why should they care about her more than she cares about herself? And by the time the others started complaining of the smell, gangrene had set in."

"Horrible, horrible," shuddered Pamela. "Remove me from this sight, life coach, I cannot bear it."

"Wait. I will show you a fourth *P* that shall vanquish all the rest."

And she breathed on the mirror just as Pamela had done.

"Now look," she said, and when Pamela gazed into the glass circle she saw an arrowy muscular sprite edged with neon, carrying in one hand a megaphone marked ASSERTIVENESS and in the other a time management chart covered in squares and dates and notes in colorful felt tip.

"This is the spirit of Proactivity," said Holly with a touch of reverence.

"All right, all right," said Pamela. "I'll join a yoga class. Today. And I have every faith it will make my shoulder better. Satisfied?" She reached into her bag for an aspirin. "Meanwhile, I'll take one of these if you don't mind."

"What other remedies do you keep in your bag?" asked Holly, peering in. "What's this painkiller for?"

"Migraine."

"That means you're resisting the flow of life. Senokot?"

"Constipation."

"What that really shows is that you're blocked. Stuck. I can help. Strepsils?"

"Sore throat."

"Do you get them often?"

"Yes."

"Ah. A sore throat means you're so angry you can't speak."

"Is that so."

"Yes. Now, Pamela, I sense you're angry. Tell me about your anger."

"Well, I do object . . . I mean, all this is very fine and upbeat, but . . . I do object, I really object . . ."

"Yes?"

"I do object to death."

"Ah," said Holly. "Death. Not really my area."

"Well, there's a lot of it about," said Pamela, wiping her eyes. "Take my word for it."

"Let us stay away from thoughts that create problems and pain," said Holly.

"It's just that it's so wasteful," continued Pamela. "And I miss my dear friends, my loved ones. I talk to them in my dreams. I tell you, Holly, it's a bone yard out there!"

"We must concentrate on the bits in between," said Holly firmly.

"Don't give me that mead hall stuff," said Pamela, blowing her nose.

"Your thoughts are making you miserable. Change your thoughts."

"It's not just death. It's suffering."

"Come now. Lighten up."

"Even if things could be put right now," said Pamela, "I don't see how it's possible to be happy, for anyone ever to be happy, when such terrible things have happened to people in history and they're dead now and nothing can be done for them."

"Remember J.O.L.L.Y.?" said the life coach. "You'll need a lighter heart if you're going to help others or indeed do anything. Turn off the news. Put on your favorite CD. All these charity leaflets you've saved—refugees, AIDS, homelessness, cruelty to children—choose one now, write a check, throw out the rest."

"Ah," said Pamela, reaching for her checkbook and studying its stubs with a pensive air. "Christmas is an expensive time."

"It certainly is," said Holly. "However, you must still write a check for a hundred pounds to the charity of your choice."

"The thing is, I've just told my daughter that I'll pay off her credit card debt—this really must be the last time—so there'll be nothing left at all."

"Then you must tell her you've changed your mind," said the life coach. "That would be very bad for her and unfair of you, encouraging her to continue spending money without thinking. Instead, book her a course with a financial therapist who will show her how to budget—I know a good one, here's his card. Then you can buy your daughter a pair of silk pajamas for Christmas, and write a nice large check to your chosen charity."

"She won't be very pleased," muttered Pamela.

"Now, what are all these piles of papers and shoeboxes full of old letters and cards?" asked Holly, ignoring this, turning her attention to the comfortless chaos surrounding them.

"Leave them alone, please," said Pamela. "These are my memories. The past."

"Clutter," said Holly. "I'm not interested in the past, and neither should you be."

"The past?" said Pamela. "It's what I am, it's what there is."

"No," said Holly, tightening her lips. "It's what there was. I tell you, you shouldn't be too interested in the past. You yourself now are the embodiment of what you have lived. What's done is done."

"But how are you to live if you don't reflect on your life?" cried Pamela.

"I have noticed that people's thoughts about the past are nearly always gloomy," said Holly. "Remorse, resentment, disappointment, these are not helpful emotions."

"Helpful?"

"Let the past go."

"So would you ban the study of history?"

"Nearly every other academic discipline has more to recommend it," said Holly. "Come, let's move on. Tell me, what do you want to happen on Christmas Day? You have asked all your relatives for lunch. How do you want the day to be?"

"I just want them to be effing well happy!" growled Pamela. "Understand? Is that too much to ask?"

"I see," said Holly. "I see. Next question: Were you good when you were little?"

"Oh, very," snapped Pamela. "No trouble at all. Good as gold. Always offering to do the washing up."

"That figures. Now, let us take another look in the psychic mirror," said Holly. "Breathe on it once more, and all will be revealed."

Again Pamela did as she was told, and presently the mist on the glass cleared to reveal a strange figure, its body puny and graceful as a child's, but with an old person's face wrinkled and withered by a thousand worries, and hair snow-white as if with age. It was sitting alone in a cold bedroom listening to an extravaganza of rage and yelling and slammed doors; it was shivering like a greyhound while it adjusted a sophisticated assemblage of sonic equipment on the little table beside it.

"Poor creature," sighed Pamela. "I don't know why but I feel sorry for it. What does its presence signify, Holly?"

"That poor creature," said Holly. "That is your inner child."

"Oh," said Pamela. "Oh dear."

"Her radar is exquisitely attuned to the moods of the adults beyond the door, and she feels responsible both for their miseries and for cheering them up."

"She's on a hiding to nowhere, then, isn't she?" said Pamela. "How idiotic."

"Idiotic," agreed Holly. "Just wanting them to be effing well happy."

"Ah," said Pamela. "Yes. I see."

She went over and sat by the fire, staring into it broodingly.

"What can I do, Holly?" she said, looking up. "What can I do to disencumber that child?"

"My time here is nearly done," said the life coach, glancing at her watch. "Now, for the final part of the program."

She took hold of Pamela's hand and led her to the door of the room.

"What is beyond this door?" she asked.

"The hall," said Pamela, mystified.

"And are there doors off the hallway?" asked Holly.

"Yes, of course," said Pamela. "Apart from the back door, there's the kitchen and the bathroom; come on, I'll show you."

She led her into the hall, which was cold and dimly lit.

"What's this low doorway here?" asked the life coach.

"That's the cupboard under the stairs."

"Show me, if you will."

"All right, but there's nothing much to see except the Hoover," said Pamela, opening the door as she was asked. Then she stopped and gasped.

"Come on in," said Holly, drawing her across the threshold and closing the door behind them.

They stood in a room whose walls were hung with boughs of bay and laurel, knots of dull-pearled mistletoe, and glossy holly branches looped with curlicues and flourishes of ivy. The polished leaves of these evergreens winked in the light of the blaze from a yule log that spat and crackled in the fireplace. Near the fire stood a stout little pine tree, its resinous fragrance filling the air, and from the branches of this tree hung garlands of sweets and tiny blown-glass trumpets and angels.

"Life coach, what is this place?" breathed Pamela, gazing round her in amazement.

"This is your Green Room for the festive season," smiled the life coach.

"Green Room? What, like the room for actors when they're not onstage?"

"Very like that," said Holly. "It is your own withdrawing room, your Green Room for twelve days. Look, did you notice that little round table laid for dinner over there? Your dinner, if I'm not mistaken."

"How delicious it looks," said Pamela, noticing the roast partridge on a nest of sliced poached pears. "Wine, too."

"I'm very pleased we found our way here, because I'll tell you now there are some of my clients whose inner children have grown so weighed down by the habits of anxiety that they don't manage to find the way back to their Green Room ever again."

"Poor them," said Pamela. "Destined never to get beyond the Hoover. Talking of inner children, though, where is mine?"

"Didn't you notice?" said the life coach. "You can't have been looking."

Pamela turned and for the first time saw the child in question, its face now smooth and wreathed in smiles, sitting on the floor in front of the fire. It was engaged in a spirited game of Scrabble with a hoary-headed ancient whose beard reached past his waist.

"Is that my inner grandfather?" she asked.

"No, that's the Old Year," said the life coach. "And look, over there beside the chimney breast, you can guess who that baby is."

She looked where she was told and saw a naked infant lying in a fur-lined basket waving its plump arms and legs in the air and crowing delightedly.

"It's the New Year, isn't it!" exclaimed Pamela; but when she turned round again the life coach had slipped away, back to the wide world web where she was needed. So she thanked the thin air instead and, smiling, joined the little family group waiting for her in front of the fire.

Constitutional

"I just think she's a bit passive-aggressive," said the woman to her friend. "In a very sweet way. D'you know what I mean?"

This is so much the sort of thing you hear on the Heath that I couldn't help smiling, straight from Stella's funeral though I was, standing aside to let them past me on to the pavement. Even five minutes later, almost at the ponds, I'm smiling, but that could be simple relief at being outside in some November sun.

The thing about a circular walk is that you end up where you started—except, of course, that you don't. My usual round trip removes me neatly from the fetid staff-room lunch hour, conveniently located as the school is on the very edge of the Heath. And as Head of Science I'm usually able to keep at least two lunch hours a week free by arranging as many of the departmental meetings and astronomy clubs and so on as I possibly can to take place after school.

Because I know exactly how long I have—quick glance at my watch, fifty-three minutes left—and exactly how long it takes, I can afford to let my mind off the lead. Look at the sparkle of that dog's urine against the dark green of the laurel, and its wolfish cocked leg. In the space of an hour I know I can walk my way back to some sort of balance after my morning-off's farewell distress before launching into sexual reproduction with Year Ten at five past two.

When the sun flares out like this, heatless and long-shadowed, the tree trunks go floodlit and even the puddles in the mud hold flashing blue snapshots of the sky. You walk past people who are so full of their lives and thoughts and talk about others, so absorbed in exchanging human information, that often their gaze stays abstractedly on the path and their legs are moving mechanically. But their dogs frisk around, curvet-ting and cantering, arabesques of pink tongues airing in their broadly smiling jaws. They bound off after squirrels or seagulls, they bark, *rowrowrow*, into the sunshine, and there is no idea anywhere of what comes next.

This walk is always the same but different, thanks to the light, the time of year, the temperature, and so on. Its sameness allows me to sink back into my thoughts as I swing along, while on the other hand I know and observe at some level that nothing is ever exactly the same as it was before.

It's reminding me of that card game my grandfather taught me, Clock Patience, this circuit, today. I'm treading the round face of a twelve-hour clock. Time is getting to be a bit of an obsession, but then I suppose that's only natural in my condition. So, it's a waiting game, Clock Patience. You deal the fifty-two cards in the pack, one for each week of the year, face down into a circle of twelve, January to December, and there is your old-fashioned clock face. I didn't find out till last week so that's something else to get used to. Stella would have been interested. Fascinated. The queen is at the top, at twelve o'clock, while the ace is low at one.

Forty-nine minutes. From that hill up there to my left it's possible to see for miles, all over London, and on a clear day I'm pretty sure I can pinpoint my road in Dalston. A skipper on the Thames looked up here at the northern heights three centuries ago and exclaimed at how even though it was midsummer the hills were capped with snow. All the Heath's low trees and bushes were festooned with clean shirts and smocks hung out to dry, white on green, this being where London's laundry was done.

So you deal the first twelve cards face down in the shape of a clock face, then the thirteenth goes, also face

147

down, into the middle. Do this three times more and you end up with four cards on every numeral and four in a line across the clock.

As I overtake an elderly couple dawdling toward the ponds, these words drift into my ears: ". . . terrible pain. Appalling. They've tried this and that but nothing seems to help. Disgusting . . ." The words float after me even though I speed up and leave the two of them like tortoises on the path behind me.

Start by lifting one of the four central cards. Is it a three of hearts? Slide it face up under the little pile at three o'clock, and help yourself to the top card there. Ten of spades? Go to ten o'clock and repeat the procedure. Ah, but when you turn up a king, the game gains pace. The king flies to the center of the clock and lies face upward. You lift his downturned neighbor and continue. Nearly always the kings beat the clock—they glare up at you from their completed gang before you have run your course, four scowling tyrants. But occasionally you get the full clock out before that happens, every hour completed—and that's very satisfying.

"Patience is more of a woman's card game," said Aidan, who prefers poker. "The secretaries at work got hooked on computer Solitaire. We had to get the IT department to wipe it from the memories."

We were lying in bed at the time.

"Have you noticed how on rush-hour trains," I

countered, "a seated man will open up his laptop in the middle of the general crush and you'll think, *He* must have important work to do. Then you peep round the edge of the screen and he's playing a game of exploding spaceships."

I don't know when I should tell him about this latest development. Pregnancy. Or even, whether.

One thing the doctor asked my grandfather to do early on, before his diagnosis, was to draw a simple clockface on a piece of paper and then sketch in the hands at five past ten. He couldn't do it. I was there. His pencil seemed to run away with him. His clock had wavy edges, it had gone into meltdown, the numerals were dropping off all over the place and the whole thing was a portrait of disintegration.

Forty-five minutes left. I can't believe my body has lasted this long, said Stella the last time I visited her in her flat. When you think (she'd said), more than ninety years, it seems quite incredible. She had few teeth, three or four perhaps, and didn't seem to mind this, although one of them came out in her sandwich that day while we were having lunch, which gave us both a shudder of horror. When she had the first of her funny turns and I visited her in the hospital, she said, "I don't care what's wrong with me. Either they put it right or not. But what's the point? Just to go on and on?"

For some reason the fact that she was ninety-three

when she died and that her body was worn out did not make her death any more acceptable to this morning's congregation. The church was rocking with indignant stifled sobs at the sight of the coffin in front of the altar, and her old body in it. She had no children but hundreds of friends. Her declared line had always been that since death is unknowable it's simply not worth thinking about. She didn't seem to derive much comfort from this at the end, though.

Prolongation of morbidity is what they're calling this new lease of life after seventy. I turned to the sharp-looking woman brushing away tears beside me in the pew this morning, and said, "You'd think it would be easier on both sides to say good-bye; but ninety-three or not, it isn't."

"That's why I won't allow myself to befriend old people anymore," said my sharp neighbor. "I can't afford to invest my time and emotion in them when the outcome's inevitable."

"That's hard!" I exclaimed.

"So's grief," she growled. "Don't give me grief. I'm not volunteering for it anymore."

Look at these benches, inscribed with the dates of the various dear departed, positioned at the side of the path so the living can rest on the dead and enjoy the view. There seems to be a new one every time I go for a walk. They're the modern version of a headstone or a sarcophagus.

"David Ford—A Kindly Man and a Good Citizen." How distant he must have been from the rest, to have this as his epitaph. Or here, equally depressing, "Marjorie Smith—Her Life Was Devotion to Others." We all know what *that* means.

The sharp woman this morning, she had a whiff of therapy-speak about her. What she said, the way she said it, reminded me of my father in some way. Let the past go, he declares; what's the point in raking over the past, chewing over old news. As my mother would say, How *convenient*. And when, precisely, does the past begin, according to him? Last year? Yesterday? A minute ago?

My father, living in Toronto at the moment, has a deliberately poor memory and refuses nostalgia point-blank. There has been a refreshing lack of clutter in the various places he's lived since leaving home when I was five. He treats his life as a picaresque adventure, sloughing off old skin and moving on, reinventing himself on a regular basis. He lives with the freshness and brutality of an infant. He can't see the point of continuity, he feels no loyalty to the past. What he values is how he feels now. That phrase, "Where are we going?," he's allergic to it, and from the moment a woman delivers herself of those words to him she's on the way out as far as he is concerned. Good-bye, Sarah, Lauren, Anna, Phoebe, and countless others, the women whom he refers to as romantic episodes.

I don't see my life in quite the same way, though I have a certain sympathy for that nonchalant approach. Aidan, for example, likes to identify his objectives and be proactive at taking life by the scruff of the neck; whereas I prefer to nose forward instinctively, toward some dim but deeply apprehended object of desire that I can't even put into words. He says that's our age difference showing, I've inherited a touch of the old hippy whereas he's free of those sentimental tendencies. Anyway, I used to say to him, what if nothing much happens to you, or lots of different disjointed things? Does that make you any less of a person? I suppose I was being aggressive-passive.

At least I was being open, unlike Aidan, who has a selective memory and failed to mention he was married. When I found out, then it was time for *me* to let the past go, to move on, despite his talk of leaving. I wasn't born yesterday.

My mother could not be more different from my father. Why they married is a mystery. She is perpetually at work on weaving the story of her life; she sees herself as the central figure in her own grand tapestry. She carries her past with her like a great snail shell, burnished with high-density embellishments. She remembers every conceivable anniversary—birthdays, deaths, first kisses, operations, house moves—and most of her talk starts with "Do you remember?" There is quite a lot I don't remember, since I left home and Scotland as soon as I could, not popular with my stepfather, the hero in her quest, her voyage-and-return after the false start that was my father. I was heavily abridged in the process. I'd be willing to bet a thousand pounds that her main concern once I tell her about the baby will be how to incorporate the role of grandmother into her carefully woven narrative. Still, Aberdeen is a long way off.

I'm finding more and more when I meet new people that, within minutes of saying hello, they're laying themselves out in front of me like scientific diagrams that they then explain, complex specimens, analyzed and summed up in their own words. They talk about their pasts in great detail, they tell me their stories, and then—this is what passes for intimacy now—they ask me to tell them mine. I have tried. But I can't. It seems cooked up, that sort of story. And how could it ever be more than the current version? It makes me feel, No, *that's* not it and *that's* not it, as soon as I've said something. Perhaps I'm my father's daughter after all. It's not that I'm particularly secretive—it's more to do with whatever it is in us that objects to being photographed.

And here's the oldest jogger I've seen for a while, barely moving, white-bearded—look, I'm going faster than him even at walking pace. It's hard not to see a bony figure at his shoulder, a figure with a scythe.

I was on the tube this morning minding my own business when I realized that the old fellow standing beside me—not quite in a walker, but bald, paunchy, in his early seventies—was giving me the eye. I looked back over my shoulder instinctively. Then I realized that it was *me* he was eyeing and couldn't restrain a shocked snort of laughter. The parameters shift once you're past forty, it seems, when it comes to the dance of wanting and being wanted. Though that was always very good with Aidan, whatever else was wrong between us, and he's seven years younger than me.

You would think that a science teacher and tutor would know how not to get pregnant. You would think so. Once again it was to do with my age. My GP noticed that I'd just had another birthday and advised me to stop taking the Pill. It was time to give my system a rest, she suggested, time to get back in touch with my natural cycle again now that I was so much less fertile because of the years. There are other methods of contraception far more natural, she continued, and far less invasive than stroke-inducing daily doses of estrogen and progestogen. She sent me off to a natural family planning guru.

I learned to chart the months, coloring my safe days in blue and my fertile days in red, in advance, thanks to the clockwork regularity of my cycle. It was pretty much half and half, with the most dangerous time from day thirteen to day seventeen, day one being the first day of my period. I took my temperature with a digital thermometer every morning and believed that I was safe once it had risen by 0.2 degrees from a previous low temperature for three days in a row. The onset of a glossy albuminous secretion, though, meant I had to be on red alert.

Emboldened by contact with my own inner calendar, its individual ebb and flow, I took a pair of compasses and made a circular chart for each monthly revolution onto tracing paper, with several inner circles all marked with the days of my private month, recording dates of orgasm, vivid dreams, time of ovulation, phases of the moon, and so on. I was steadier and more pedestrian during the first half of my inner month, I noticed—and more thin-skinned, clever, and volatile, in the fortnight before my period.

When after several months I placed the translucent sheets of tracing paper on top of one another, I was able to see both the regularly repeated events and also the slight variations over time as a wheeling overlap, so that looking back down the past year was like gazing into a helix with seashell striations.

"My cycle seems rather disturbed," I said to the Wise Woman at one of our consultations.

"Two teaspoons of honey daily should regularize that," she said. And I nodded and smiled. No kidding. Me, with a biology degree from a good university and a keen interest in neuroscience. Then, of course, three weeks after saying good-bye forever to Aidan, I found I was pregnant. Talk about the biological clock.

Thirty-six minutes left. See the sun on the bark of this sweet chestnut tree, and how it lights up the edges of these spiraling wrinkled grooves. Our brain cortex looks like wet tree bark, as I was telling Year Eleven only yesterday. This expansive outer layer with its hundred billion nerve cells has to contract itself into tightly concertinaed ripples and ridges, it has to pleat and fold back on itself in order to pack down far enough to fit inside the skull.

It's hard to think of Stella this morning in her coffin, her bones, her skull with the brain annihilated. She could remember ninety years ago, as many nonagenarians can, as though it were yesterday; but—unusual, this—she could also remember yesterday. That is a great thing in extreme old age, to be both near- and far-sighted. Once I asked her what was her earliest memory, and she thought it might have been when she was one or possibly two, sitting outside the post office in her pram on a snowy day. She was watching the boy in the pram on the other side of the doorway as he howled and howled—"And I thought, 'Oh do be quiet! They're coming back, you know. It's really ridiculous to make a noise like that. They haven't left us here forever.' He was wearing a white fur bonnet that I wanted for myself."

This memory of hers sent some messenger running in my brain, zigzagging along corridors and byways of the mind, and triggered the retrieval of my own earliest memory, which she heard with a hoot of incredulity. I was standing outside my parents' bedroom door, and for the first time felt flood over me the realization that they were not part of me. They were separate. And I thought of my own selfish demands, and wanted to go in to them and say how sorry I was for being a burden to them and how considerate they would find me now that I had realized I was not part of them. The bedroom door was tall as a tree in front of me.

"Very guilty," I told Stella. "I feel guilty generally. Don't you?"

She paused and we both waited to see what she would come up with. Talking to her was like mackerel fishing, the short wait and then the flash of silver.

"I don't feel guilty *enough*," she said, with emphasis, at last.

When her doorbell rang, she would open the front room window of her first-floor flat and let down a fishing line with a key attached to the end of it where the hook would otherwise have been. That way her visitors could unlock the front door and let themselves in, saving her the stairs.

She listened with interest while I tried to describe the latest theories about memory, how they now think that when you try to remember something you are not going to your mental library to take a memory book off the shelf or to play back a memory video. No, you are remembering the original memory; you are reconstructing that memory. The more frequently you chase a particular memory and reconstruct it, the more firmly established in the brain that memory track becomes.

This shortcut I've just taken—thirty-one minutes, I'm watching the time—at first it was nothing but that the grass had been walked on once or twice; but now it's obviously been trodden over again and again, hundreds of times, and has become an established path. Repetition—repeated reconstruction of the memory—strengthens it.

"So, Stella," I said, "you remember that fur bonnet from ninety years ago because you've remembered it so often that by now it's an established right of way, it's on all your maps."

"I am not aware of having called up that memory more than once or twice," said Stella. "In fact I could have sworn it appeared for the first time last week. But you may be right."

Occasional Bentleys used to glide down our mean street and disgorge a superannuated star or two—a fabled ex-Orsino, a yesteryear Hamlet. Stella had been a well-known actress, she had traveled the world with various theater companies, she had never married; nor apparently had she ever made much money, for here she was in extreme old age living in a rented room on next to nothing. She was still working, for heaven's sake. Three times a week she would creep painfully down the stairs a step at a time, allowing a good twenty minutes for the descent, then wait for the bus to take her into Gower Street, where she introduced her students to Beatrice and Imogen and Portia and the traditional heartbeat of the iambic pentameter. She remained undimmed, without any of the usual inward-turning self-protective solipsism, open like a Shakespearean heroine to grief and chance and friendship even in her tenth decade.

If it is true that each established memory makes a track, a starry synaptic trail in the brain, and that every time we return to (or, as they insist, *reconstruct*) that particular constellation of memory, we strengthen it, then so is the following. Stella's billion lucent constellations may have been extinguished at her death, but she herself has become part of my own brain galaxy, and part of the nebulous clusters of all her myriad friends. Every time I remember Stella, I'll be etching her deeper into myself, my cells, my memory.

Twenty-nine minutes until I'm due back at school. That staff room yesterday was like a rest home for the elderly. The young ones had all gone off to leap around at some staff-pupil netball match, leaving the over-thirties to spread out with their sandwiches. I sat marking at a table near where Max, Head of Math, was chatting with Lower School History Peter and the new Geography woman.

"It's on the tip of my tongue," said Max, his eyes locking hungrily onto Peter's. "You know, the one that looks like . . ."

"In Year Eight?" said Peter.

"Bloody hell, I've got that thing," groaned Max, "you know, that disease, what the hell's it called, where you can't remember anything . . ."

"No, you haven't!" snapped Peter. He fancies him.

"I went to get some money out on Sunday," he fretted. "I stood in the queue for the cash machine for ten minutes, then when it was my turn I couldn't remember my PIN number. I'm Head of Math, for pity's sake. So I tapped in 1989—in case I'd used my memorable date, because that's it—but apparently I hadn't because the machine then swallowed my card."

"You read about people being tortured for their PIN numbers," said the new Geography woman—what *is* her name?—"well, they could torture me to within an inch of my life and I still wouldn't know it. I'd be dead and they still wouldn't have the money."

"What happened in 1989?" asked Peter keenly.

"Arsenal beat Liverpool two nil at Anfield," said Max.

"Did they?" said Peter.

"You're not into football, then," said Max as he turned to the crossword, shaking out his newspaper, and Peter's face fell.

It reminded me of that scene in the restaurant last

time I was out for a meal with Aidan. The couple at the neighboring table were gaping at each other wordlessly, silent with frustration. Then he electrified everyone within earshot by softly howling, "It's gone, it's gone." I thought he'd swallowed a tooth, an expensive crown. His expression seemed to bear this out—anguish and a mute plea for silence. But no—it was merely that he had forgotten what he was halfway through saying. He was having a senior moment.

I've always had a very good memory. It used to be that any word I wanted would fly to me like a bird, I'd put my hand up and pluck it out of the air. Effortless. Gratifying. Facts, too, came when called, and when someone gave me his phone number I would be able to hold it in my head till later when I had a pen—even several hours later.

Thanks to this, I never had any trouble with exams, unlike my GP cousin who spent her years at medical school paddling round frantically in a sea of mnemonics. "Two Zulus Buggered My Cat," she'd say. "Test me, I've got to learn the branches of the facial nerve." And what was the one she found so hideously embarrassing? See if I can remember. It was the one for the cranial nerves.

Oh	Optic
Oh	Olfactory
Oh	Oculomotor
To	Trochlear

Touch	Trigeminal
And	Abducent
Feel	Facial
Veronica's	Vestibulocochlear
Glorious	Glossopharyngeal
Vagina	Vagus
And	Accessory
Hymen	Hypoglossal

Not that she's prudish, but she was in a predominantly male class of twenty-two-year-olds at the time, and that's her name—Veronica.

The minute I hit forty, I lost that instant recall. I had to wait for the right cue, listen to the cogs grinding, before the word or fact would come to me. Your brain cells are dying off, Aidan would taunt.

Even so, I sometimes think my memory is too good. I don't forget *enough*. I wish I could forget *him*. It's all a question of emotional metabolism, whether you're happy or not. You devour new experience, you digest and absorb what will be nourishing, you let the rest go. And if you can't shed waste matter, you'll grow costive and gloomy and dyspeptic. My mother always says she can forgive (with a virtuous sigh); but she can never forget (with a beady look). She is mistaken in her pride over this. Not to be able to forget is a curse. I read somewhere a story that haunted me, about a young man, not particularly clever or remarkable in any way except that he remembered everything that he had ever seen or heard. The government of whatever country it was he lived in grew interested, thinking this might be useful to them, but nothing came of it. The man grew desperate, writing out sheets of total recall and then setting fire to them in the hope that seeing them go up in flames would raze them from his mind. Nothing worked. He was a sea of unfiltered memories. He went mad.

Max is worried that forgetting his PIN number is the first step to losing his mind, but really his only problem is that he knows too much. How old is he? Near retirement, anyway. Twenty years older than me. After a certain age your hard disk is much fuller than it's ever been, thanks to the buildup of the years. Mine has certainly started refusing to register anything it doesn't regard as essential—I frequently find myself walking back down the road now to check I've locked the front door behind me. Your internal organs stop self-renewing at a certain point, and at the same time your mind begins to change its old promiscuous habits in the interests of managing what it's already got.

I sometimes taunt Max with the crossword if I'm sitting near him in the staff room during the lunch hour. "It's on the tip of my tongue," he moans. Last week there was a brilliant clue, tailor-made for a mathematician, too: "Caring, calm, direct—New Man's sixty-third year. (5,11; 9 Across and 3 Down)." He rolled his eyes and scowled and moaned, followed various trails up blind alleys, barked with exasperation, and his mind ran around all over the place following various scents. It was interesting to observe him in the act.

Twenty-five minutes, and I've reached the tangled old oak near the top fence with its scores of crooked branches and thousands of sharp-angled twigs. I use trees to help when I'm explaining to my sixth-form biologists how the brain works. "Neurons are the brain's thinking cells," I say, and they nod. "There are billions of neurons in everyone's brain," I say, and they nod and smile. "And each one of these billions of neurons is fringed with thousands of fine whiskers called dendrites," I continue, while they start to look mildly incredulous—and who can blame them? The word *dendrite* comes from the Greek for tree, I tell them, and our neuron-fringing dendrites help create the brain's forest of connectivity. Dendrites are vital messengers between neuron and neuron, they cross the little gappy synapses in between, they link our thoughts together. It's as though several hundred thousand trees have been uprooted and had their heads pushed together from every direction—there is an enormous interlocking tangle of branches and touching twigs.

While I waited for Max as he wrestled with that clue, I could almost hear the rustle and creak of trees conferring. "I'll give you another clue," I said. "You're in it." But even that didn't help him.

It's not that my mind is going, it's more like my long-term memory is refusing to accept any more material unless it's really unmissable. When I was young I remembered everything because it was all new. I could remember whether I'd locked the door because I'd locked it only a few hundred times before. Now I can't ever remember whether I've locked it as I've done it thousands of times and my memory will no longer deign to notice what is so old and stale.

My short-term memory is in fact wiping the slate clean disconcertingly often these days. Like an autocratic secretary, it decides whether to let immediate thoughts and impressions cross over into the long-term memory's library—or whether to press the DELETE button on them. "I've got an enormous backlog of filing and I simply can't allow yet more unsifted material to accumulate," it snaps, peering over its bifocals. "It's not that there isn't enough space—there is—but it's gotten to the point where I need to sort and label carefully before shelving, or it'll be lost forever—it'll be in there somewhere, but irretrievable."

The thing about my sixth-formers—about all my pupils, in fact—is that it is not necessary for them to commit anything to memory. Why should they store information in their skulls when they've got it at their fingertips? Yet Stella's decades of learning speeches by heart meant that when age began its long war of attrition her mind was shored up with great heaps of blank verse. I have noticed myself that if I don't continue to learn by repetition, even just the odd phone number, then my ability to do so starts to slide away. I will not, however, be trying to learn Russian in my old age as I once promised myself. No, I'll follow the progress of neuroscientific research, wherever it's got to. I've learned from Jane Blizzard's example that you have to find a way to graft new stuff onto old in order to make it stick.

My ex-colleague Jane had been teaching French and Latin for as long as anyone could remember. She decided when she took early retirement at fifty-five last year that she wanted to study for the three sciences at A-level, and came to me for help in organizing this. Forty years ago she had not been allowed to take science at her all-girls school, even at a lower level, and felt this was a block of ignorance she wanted to melt. She's clever, and passed the three A-levels with flying colors, but to her horror discovered a few months later that all her newly acquired knowledge had trickled away. She had not been able to attach it to anything she already knew, and her long-term memory had refused to retain it.

As I overtake a couple of pram-pushing mothers in their early thirties, I hear "Her feet were facing the wrong way." Would this mean anything to a girl of seventeen? Or to a man of sixty-three? My pupils will balk at my pregnancy. The younger ones will find it positively disgusting. I speed up and pass two older women, late fifties perhaps, free of makeup, wrapped in a jumble of colored scarves and glasses on beaded chains, escorting a couple of barrel-shaped labradors as big as buses. "She was just lying on the pavement panting, refusing to move," one of them announces as I pass. They have moved on from the dramas of children to the life-and-death stuff of dogs. And I, I who am supposed to be somewhere between these two stages, where am *I* in this grand pageant? My colleagues will say to one another, So why didn't she get rid of it?

Eighteen minutes left, and I'm making good time. If I'm lucky I might even catch Max groaning over his unsolved clues and help put him out of his misery.

It was my grandfather again who introduced me to crosswords—first the general knowledge ones, then, as I left childhood, the cryptics. He had an acrobatic mind and a generous nature. I used to stay with him and my grandmother for long stretches of the school holidays, as we liked one another's company and my parents were otherwise involved.

When my grandfather started to forget at the age of eighty-one—by which time I had long since finished at university and was on to my second teaching job—it was not the more usual benign memory loss. It was because his short-term memory, his mind's secretary, was being smothered and throttled by a tangle of rogue nerve fibers.

Since different sorts of memory are held in different parts of the brain, the rest stayed fine for a while. He could tell me in detail about his schooldays, but not remember that his beloved dog had died the day before. It reminded me of the unsinkable *Titanic* with its separate compartments. In time his long-term memory failed as well. The change was insidious and incremental, but I noticed it sharply as there would usually be several months between my visits.

Talking to someone whose short-term memory has gone is like pouring liquid into a baseless vessel. Your words go in then straight through without being held at all. That really is memory like a sieve. While I was digging the hole in his back garden in which to bury the dog, he stood beside me and asked what I was doing.

"Poor Captain was run over," I replied, "so I'm digging his grave."

"Oh, that's terrible," he exclaimed, tears reddening his rheumy old eyes. "How terrible! How did it happen?"

I described how Captain's body had been found at the curbside on the corner of Blythedale Avenue, but he was examining the unraveled cuff of his cardigan by the time I'd finished.

"What's this hole you're digging, then?" he asked, a

moment or two after I'd told him; and I told him again, marveling to see new grief appear in his eyes. As often as he asked I answered, and each time his shocked sorrow about the dog was raw and fresh. How exhausting not to be able to digest your experience, to be stalled on the threshold of your own inner life. For a while he said that he was losing himself, and then he lost that.

Finding his way back into a time warp some fifty years before, he one night kicked my terrified old grandmother out of bed because, he said, his parents would be furious at finding him in bed with a stranger.

"I'm not a stranger," she wept. "I'm your wife."

"You say so," he hissed at her, widening his eyes, then narrowing them to slits. "But I know better."

From then on, he was convinced that she was an impostor, a crafty con artist who fooled everybody except himself into thinking that she was his eighty-year-old wife.

In the evenings he would start to pace up and down the length of their short hallway, muttering troubled words to himself, and after an hour or so of this he would take the kettle from the kitchen and put it in the airing cupboard on the landing, or grab a favorite needlepoint cushion from the sofa and craftily smuggle it into the microwave. He wrote impassioned incomprehensible letters in their address book, and forgot the names of the most ordinary things. I mean, *really* forgot them. "I want the thing there is to drink out of," he shouted when the word *cup* left him. He talked intimately about his childhood to the people on the television screen. He got up to fry eggs in the middle of the night. He accused me of stealing all their tea towels.

"I want to go home," he wept.

"But you *are* home," howled my grandmother.

"And who the hell are *you*?" he demanded, glaring at her in unfeigned dismay.

But, because muscle memories are stored in quite another part of the brain, the cerebellum at the back, he was still able to sit at the piano and play Debussy's *L' isle joyeuse* with unnerving beauty.

Thirteen minutes. It always surprises me how late in the year the leaves stay worth looking at. November gives the silver birches real glamour, a shower of gold pieces at their feet and still they keep enough to clothe them, thousands of tiny lozenge-shaped leaves quaking on their separate stems. That constant tremor made them unpopular in the village where I grew up—palsied, they called them.

Trees live for a long time, much longer than we do. Look at this oak, so enormous and ancient standing in the center of the leaf-carpeted clearing, it must be more than five hundred years old. It's an extremely slow developer, the oak, and doesn't produce its first acorn until it's over sixty. Which makes me feel better about the elderly prima gravida label.

They have been known to live for a thousand years, oak trees, and there are more really old ones growing on the Heath than in the whole of France. Look at it standing stoutly here, all elbows and knees. When the weather is stormy, they put up signs round here— BEWARE OF FALLING LIMBS. It was these immensely strong and naturally angled branches, of course, which gave the Elizabethans the crucks they needed for their timber-framed houses and ships.

Stella was like seasoned timber, she stayed strong and flexible almost until the end. When she had her second stroke, three weeks after the first, she was taken to a nursing home for veterans of the stage and screen, some-where out in Middlesex. In the residents' lounge sat the old people who were well enough to be up. They looked oddly familiar. I glanced round and realized that I was recognizing the blurred outlines of faces I had last seen ten times the size and seventy years younger. Here were the quondam matinee idols and femmes fatales of my grandparents' youth.

Then I went to Stella's room. I held her strong long hand and it was a bundle of twigs in mine. There was an inky bruise to the side of her forehead. Her snowy hair had been tied in a little topknot with narrow white satin ribbon.

I talked, and talked on; I said I'd assume she understood everything—"Squeeze my hand if you can to agree"—and felt a small pressure. I talked about Shakespeare and the weather and food and any other silly thing that came into my head. Her blue eyes gazed at me with such frustration—she couldn't move or speak, she was locked in—that I said, "Patience, dear Stella. It's the only way."

Her face caved in on itself, a theatrical mask of grief. Her mouth turned into a dark hole round her toothless gums, a tear squeezing from her old agonized eyes, and she made a sad keening hooting noise.

Afterward, in the corridor, I stood and cried for a moment, and the matron gave me automatic soothing words.

"Not to worry," I said. "I'm not even a relative. It's just the pity of it."

"Yes, yes," she said. "The pity of it, to be sure. Ah, but during the week I nurse on a cancer ward, and some of those patients having to leave their young families . . ."

I really did not want to have to think about untimely death on top of everything else, and certainly not in my condition; so I returned to the subject of Stella.

"Walled up in a failed body," I said. "Though perhaps it would be worse to be sound in body but lost in your mind, dipping in and out of awareness of your own lost self. Which is worse?"

"Ah well, we are not to have the choice anyway," she

said, glancing at her watch. "We cannot choose when the time comes."

The trouble is, old age has moved on. Three score years and ten suddenly looks a bit paltry, and even having to leave at eighty would make us quite indignant these days. Sixty is now the crown of middle age. And have you noticed how ancient the parents of young children are looking? Portly, grizzled, groaning audibly as their backs creak while they lean over to guide tiny scooters and bicycles, it's not just angst at the work-life balance that bows them down. Last time I stopped for a cup of tea at the café over by the bandstand, I saw a lovely new baby in the arms of a white-haired matriarch. Idly I anticipated the return of its mother from the ladies and looked forward to admiring a generational triptych. Then the baby started to grizzle, and the woman I'd taken for its grandmother unbuttoned her shirt and gave it her breast. No, it's not disgust or ridicule I felt, nothing remotely like—only adjustment. And of course that will probably be me next year.

My baby is due early in summer, according to their dates and charts. If it arrives before July, I'll still be forty-three. Who knows, I might be only halfway through; it's entirely possible that I'll live to be eighty-six. How times change. My mother had me at thirty-two, and she will become a grandmother at seventy-five. Her mother had her at twenty-one, and became a grandmother at fifty-three. At this rate my daughter will have her own first baby at fifty-four and won't attain grandmotherhood until she's a hundred and nineteen.

I'd better take out some life insurance. I hadn't bothered until now because if I died, well, I'd be dead so I wouldn't be able to spend it. But it has suddenly become very necessary. I can see that. Maternity leave and when to take it; childminders, nurseries, commuting against the clock; falling asleep over marking; not enough money, no trees in Dalston; the lure of Cornwall or Wales. I've seen it all before. But it's possible with just the one, I've seen that, too.

I'm not quite into the climacteric yet, that stretch from forty-five to sixty when the vital force begins to decline; or so they used to say. And a climacteric year was one that fell on an odd multiple of seven (so, seven, twenty-one, thirty-five, and so on), which brings me back to my glee at that crossword clue last week, and the way I taunted old Max with it: "Caring, calm, direct—New Man's sixty-third year (5,11; 9 Across and 3 Down)." Grand climacteric, of course. The grand climacteric, the sixty-third year, a critical time for men in particular.

To think that my grandfather had three more decades after *that*. Toward the end of his very long life—like Stella, he lived to ninety-three—it was as though he was being rewound or spooled in. He became increasingly childish, stamping his feet in tantrums, gobbling packets of Jelly Babies and fairy cakes, demanding to be read aloud to from *The Tale of Two Bad Mice*. He needed help with dressing and undressing, and with everything else. Then he became a baby again, losing his words, babbling, forgetting how to walk, lying in his cot crying. Just as he had once grown toward independence, so, with equal gradualness, he now reverted to the state of a newborn. Slowly he drifted back down that long corridor with fluttering curtains. At the very end, if you put your finger in the palm of his hand, he would grasp it, as a baby does, grab it, clutch at it. When at last he died, his memory was as spotless as it had been on the day he first came into the world.

Seven minutes left, and I'll pause here at the home-run ash tree to pull off a bunch of keys, as children do, for old time's sake. So ingenious, these winged seeds drying into twists that allow them to spin far from the tree in the wind; nothing if not keen to propagate. I have a particular liking for this ash tree; it's one of my few regular photographic subjects.

I'm careful how I take photographs. I've noticed how you can snap away and fail to register what you're snapping; you can take a photograph of a scene instead of looking at it and making it part of you. If you weren't careful, you could have whole albums of the years and hardly any memories of them.

I take my camera onto the Heath, but only on the first of the month, and then I take only the same twelve photographs. That is, I stand in exactly the same twelve places each time—starting with the first bench at the ponds and ending with this ash tree—and photograph the precise same views. At the end of the year I line up the twelves in order, the February dozen beneath the January dozen and so on, and in the large resultant square the year waxes and wanes. You don't often catch time at work like this. Aidan was quite intrigued, and soon after we met he was inspired to add a new Monday morning habit on his way to work. He left five minutes early, then paused to sit in the kiosk near the exit at Baker Street to have four of those little passport photos taken. He stuck these weekly records into a scrapbook, and after eighteen months it was nearly full. It was what I asked for in September when I found out that he already had a wife and child. He refused. So, in a rage, I took it. I was going to give it back, it belonged to him; but now, clearly, it doesn't belong to him in the same way anymore. It's his baby's patrimony.

I have a feeling that this baby will be a girl. In which case, of course, I'll call her Stella. If the dates are accurate, then she'll be born in early summer. I might well be pushing her along this very path in a pram by then, everything green and white around us, with all the leaves out and the nettles and cow parsley six feet high.

Four minutes to go, and I'm nearly there. Walking round the Heath on days like this when there is some color and sun, I can feel it rise in me like mercury in a thermometer, enormous deep delight in seeing these old trees with their last two dozen leaves worn like earrings, amber and yellow and crimson, and in being led off by generously lit paths powdered silver with frost. It must be some form of benign forgetfulness, this rising bubble of pleasure in my chest, at being here, now, part of the landscape and not required to do anything but exist. I feel as though I've won some mysterious game.

Two minutes to spare, and I'm back where I started, off the path and onto the pavement. That got the blood circulation moving. It's not often that I beat the four scowling kings. There's the bell. Just in time.

A Note on the Type

This book was set in Fairfield, a typeface designed by the distinguished American artist and engraver Rudolph Ruzicka (1883–1978). In its structure Fairfield displays the sober and sane qualities of the master craftsman whose talents were dedicated to clarity. Ruzicka was born in Bohemia and came to America in 1894. He designed and illustrated many books, and was the creator of a considerable list of individual prints in a variety of techniques.

Composed by Stratford Publishing Services,
Brattleboro, Vermont
Printed and bound by R. R. Donnelley & Sons,
Harrisonburg, Virginia
Designed by Anthea Lingeman